# Even Odder

## More Stories to Chill the Heart

# STEVE BURT

### Illustrations by
### Jessica Hagerman

Bur'
Cr₁

Norw

D1410117

# Even Odder
## More Stories to Chill the Heart

FIRST EDITION

Copyright © 2003 by
Steven E. Burt

Second Printing 2005

ISBN 10       0-9741407-0-8
ISBN 13     978-0-9741407-0-4

Printed in USA

Inquiries should be addressed to:

*Burt Creations*

Steve Burt
29 Arnold Place
Norwich, CT 06360

T  866-693-6936
F  860-889-4068
www.burtcreations.com

Illustrations by Jessica Hagerman
Design by Dotti Albertine

# Rants and Raves for Steve Burt

➤ Bram Stoker Award for Young Adults 2004
➤ 3 Ray Bradbury Creative Writing Awards
➤ 7 Honorable Mentions, Year's Best Fantasy & Horror
➤ Best Mystery/Suspense, Benjamin Franklin Award (silver)
➤ Best Horror Book (Hon. Mention), *ForeWord* Award
➤ Best Genre Fiction (runner-up) and Best Inspirational (runner-up), *Writer's Digest* 10th International Self-Published Book Awards
➤ Book of the Year Finalist, *ForeWord* Award
➤ Bram Stoker Award Nominee/Finalist 2003
➤ *ForeWord* Best Juvenile/Young Adult Book (Finalist)

*Steve Burt has a taste for chilling the heart. His prose is genuine and well constructed. It relies more on atmosphere and skillful plotting than blood and gore, making his stories old-fashioned in the best sense of the term. If you think, "they just don't write them like that anymore," you'll be pleased to discover that Burt does.*
— GARRETT PECK, THE HELLNOTES BOOK REVIEW

*Steve Burt has a firm grasp of the unsettling and the uncanny . . . His stories are set in a recognizable world, but they never go in the obvious direction, preferring instead to take off down dark alleys and twisting roads which leave the reader shivering and looking nervously into dark corners when the book is closed.*
— BARBARA RODEN, EDITOR, *ALL HALLOWS*
(THE MAGAZINE OF THE GHOST STORY SOCIETY)

*If ever there was an author to rival the storytelling genius of M.R. James and E.F. Benson, Steve Burt is it. Eerie and compelling, Burt's prose will have you relishing those lonely places where light dare not tread.*
— DON H. LAIRD, PUBLISHER, *CROSSOVER PRESS,*
*THRESHOLD MAGAZINE*

# Thanks to

. . . Jessica Hagerman for the great cover art and illustrations.

. . . Dotti Albertine of Albertine Book Design, Santa Monica, CA, who took my rudimentary ideas and designed the front and back covers and the book's interior.

. . . Ellen Reid, book shepherd extraordinaire, who saw my potential as a popular author and served not only as ramrod for my first projects, but helped organize my publishing business overall.

. . . My wife Jo Ann and daughter Wendy for their constant support and encouragement and for being each story's first readers. Special thanks to Wendy for proofreading, editing, challenging, and suggesting.

# About the Artist

JESSICA E. HAGERMAN is a freelance illustrator who works primarily in pen and ink. She lives in Three Rivers, Massachusetts with her cat Simon. Jessie did the cover and illustrations for *Odd Lot* (*Even Odder's* predecessor), which won three awards. In addition to illustrating CD jackets, books, and occasional medical articles, Jessie uses her degree in Art Therapy to work with children at Shriners Children's Hospital in Springfield, Massachusetts. She also plays guitar and sings, and is a co-proprietor of Peaceful Products.

# About the Author

Since 1979 Steve Burt has been a pastor, a professor, and a popular keynote speaker, mixing humor and stories in with his teaching. In fact, if there's a thread that weaves its way through his distinguished career, it's his storytelling. Steve Burt is a master storyteller.

In 1983 Steve received a Masters from Bangor Theological Seminary, and in 1987 he graduated at the top of his doctoral class at Andover Newton Theological School. After that he wrote two best-selling church leadership books and a handful of others.

Then, at the end of 2000, his *A Christmas Dozen: Christmas Stories to Warm the Heart* sold enough copies by word-of-mouth in its first 40 days and 40 nights to replace his yearly pastor's salary. Requests poured in for "New England's Christmas Story Pastor" to read at churches, senior centers, and on radio. *Writer's Digest* named *A Christmas Dozen* runner-up for **Year's Best Inspirational Book** and *ForeWord Magazine* named it a finalist for Book of the Year.

On May 5, 2001, his 52nd birthday, Rev. Dr. Burt "retired" from pastoral ministry to pursue a calling as a full-time writer/storyteller. By the end of that year—calling them his "light side" and his "dark side"—he produced two more story collections: *Unk's Fiddle: Stories to Touch the Heart* and *Odd Lot: Stories to Chill the Heart*.

*Odd Lot* was even more surprising. It earned awards in the categories: **Best Genre Fiction Book, Best Horror Book,** and **Best Mystery/Suspense Book**. Six stories earned honorable mentions in **Year's Best Fantasy & Horror**. Reader response was so strong that Steve wrote the sequel, *Even Odder: More Stories to Chill the Heart* in winter/spring 2003. It was a 2003 **Bram Stoker Nominee** and wound up runnerup to Harry Potter. In 2004 *Oddest Yet* won the **Stoker for Young Adults** by tying Clive Barker's *Abarat*. *Wicked Odd,* fourth in the series, hit shelves in July 2005.

# Also by Steve Burt

*Wicked Odd, Still More Stories to Chill the Heart*
Burt Creations 2005

*Oddest Yet, Even More Stories to Chill the Heart*
Burt Creations 2004

*Odd Lot, Stories to Chill the Heart*
Burt Creations 2001

*A Christmas Dozen, Christmas Stories to Warm the Heart*
Burt Creations 2000 (paperback)
2001 (audiobook) 2002 (hardcover)

*The Little Church That Could, Raising Small Church Esteem*
Judson Press 2000

*Unk's Fiddle, Stories to Touch the Heart*
Steven E. Burt 1995 (hardcover)
Burt Creations 2001 (paperback)

*What Do You Say to a Burning Bush? Sermons for the Season After Pentecost*, CSS Publishing 1995

*My Lord, He's Loose in the World! Meditations on the Meaning of Easter*
Brentwood Christian Press 1994

*Raising Small Church Esteem* with Hazel Roper
Alban Institute 1992

*Christmas Special Delivery, Stories and Meditations for Christmas*
Fairway Press 1991

*Fingerprints on the Chalice, Contemporary Communion Meditations*
CSS Publishing 1990

*Activating Leadership in the Small Church Clergy and Laity Working Together*, Judson Press 1988

# Introduction

*Even Odder: More Stories to Chill the Heart,* is the sequel to *Odd Lot: Stories to Chill the Heart.* It is the result of two things: (1) reader demand for more "odd" stories; and (2) a storytelling / writing experiment.

*Odd Lot* (October 2001) was a 9-story collection of my previously published stories, including 6 that had won Honorable Mentions in the **Year's Best Fantasy & Horror.** It went on to win a **Benjamin Franklin Award** for **Best Mystery/Suspense Book** (silver medal), **Best Horror Book** (Sole Honorable Mention) at the *ForeWord Magazine* Awards, and was a runner-up for **Best Genre Fiction** at *Writer's Digest's* 10th International Self-Published Book Awards. *Odd Lot* quickly went through 4 printings and readers wrote to ask for more.

As an experiment to help overcome my January 2003 writer's block (the dreaded blank page), I shifted from story writing back to story telling, a mode responsible for several of the better read-aloud tales in *Odd Lot.* For six weeks I carried a micro-cassette recorder with me on my hour-long morning walk with my dog Opie. Every day, shortly after the start of our walk, at the edge of a certain meadow, I'd stop and close my eyes, looking/listening for an opening line. No matter how good or bad it was, I'd latch onto it and start speaking as I walked. I had no preconceived story idea and no inkling where the tale might lead me. It was both terrifying and exciting.

In March, while addressing Children's Literature students at Fitchburg State College in Massachusetts, I played a little of one of those tapes. The students didn't hear a smooth tale—nothing at all like the polished stories from *Odd Lot.* What they heard was the labored breathing of a hiker, the crunch of crusty snow underfoot, the journey—and the choppy story—interrupted by the hiker's commands to his dog and greetings to passersby. The students heard a story being birthed—with all the the lulls and pauses, the contractions, the bearing down, the pain and anguish. They heard me in my dual role as mother and midwife, and they heard a new creation—one hidden from view for who knows how many eons—rasping and gasping and gulping its first breaths of air as it fought to survive the light of day.

Later I read them the smoothed-out, transcribed/edited/printed version of the same story. They loved it.

That 6-week experiment allowed me to rediscover the magic and joy of making up stories orally, the way our family did on car trips, when we took turns adding a sentence to a growing story and watched it take shape the way a braided rug does. And I learned anew something even the best writers forget from time to time—how the rhythm, the flow, of a story has a life of its own and will help you to complete it—will insist upon it. I found, too, that sometimes a story must be told aloud first, before it is written down and eventually read or spoken aloud again.

I learned too about writers' and storytellers' faith—about trusting the source/muse from which stories come. As Yoda advised Luke Skywalker in *Star Wars: Trust The Force.*

It worked. Out of the experiment came 33 spanking-new stories. Sixteen I transcribed to disk between March 15 and April 30. The first, "The Praying Man," was a macabre mainstream story that won **Honorable Mention** at the 2003 Ray Bradbury Creative Writing Awards. The other 15, all original and until now unpublished, are presented here for your enjoyment as *Even Odder.*

If *Even Odder* thrives the way *Odd Lot* has, the third addition to the Odd family will soon be on its way. I think I'll name it *Oddest Yet.*

# EVEN ODDER
## More Stories to Chill the Heart

# CONTENTS

# John Flynn's Banshee

John Flynn—everyone called him Jack—stepped away from the window. He'd seen the hearse go by two or three times now, an older model, black one. This wasn't the first time he'd seen it on this street in the Irish section of town. It made him nervous. When the hearse came around in the evening—it was now six o'clock—it wasn't for a funeral; it was always to pick up a body. It meant someone had been called in. Usually the police cars were at a house first. Perhaps someone had died in bed or been found on the floor, an older person with a hip broken in a fall who had stayed there for a day or two with no way to call for help. A newspaper carrier or a mail carrier might have noticed the newspapers or mail hadn't been picked up for a couple of days and phoned the cops. That was the only reason the old black hearse would come cruising through the neighborhood this time of night.

Jack took his seat at the supper table as his wife began putting out the various dishes: a thick beef stew, homemade coleslaw, buttermilk biscuits. While she dished it up, he rifled through a stack of mail. He had only gotten home from his factory job a few minutes before—after the usual stop at the bar for a few drinks and a couple of games of darts with the boys—just in time for supper. He passed the John Flynn mail across the table to his father and kept the John Flynn II mail for himself.

# Even Odder ✱ STEVE BURT

The white-haired man across the table was in his eighties, but he certainly wasn't on his last legs. With his crooked pug nose and scar over one eyebrow from a pub brawl, the old man still looked tough as a tree stump. When Jack was young, the old man had beaten him with a belt, a coat hanger, a wooden paddle, even a barber's thick razor strop. He'd been a tough disciplinarian who beat his son until he was eighteen. And then it was as if Jackie was suddenly an adult—Jack—and the old man stopped hitting him.

Now Jack was 50 and had a young wife of 30, Tina. She stood by the stove cooking, with their toddler Maria on her hip. The girl was their firstborn and started out colicky, which Jack took to be simply a terrible temper, which enraged him. But he found ways to keep her in line. Not the strop yet—it was too early for that—but the bare hands on the buttocks and the little finger flicks—plink, plink—on the face. She was learning.

A cry came from the bedroom. The four-month-old was awake now, John III. Johnny, they were calling him, to distinguish the father, the son, and the grandson: John the first, the second, the third.

When everything was on the table, Tina sat down at one end of it, depositing Maria in her high chair. No one moved. They all knew the routine. It was time for grace, something John the patriarch—King John I, Maria called him behind his back—would pronounce. He did it every night. If anyone made the mistake of reaching for a biscuit, or started to serve the stew or the coleslaw before the grace, it meant a whack on the hand, either from John—King John I—or from Jack—King John II. Jack was the heir apparent, although nothing seemed that apparent, for although old King John I had suffered a heart attack only a few months before, he didn't appear any closer to departing the earthly realm for the heavenly, if he had a chance of going there at all.

"I might prefer to go where it's warmer," he'd often said jokingly, except there wasn't much humor in his voice. It was the humor of a tyrant. And yet, tyrant that he was, Jack felt some sort of feeling for his father. He didn't know whether it was love or fear, but certainly not admiration.

Then again, perhaps it was admiration; the old man had held the family together when Jack's mother died when he was barely twelve. She had taken a fall down the stairs late one night when she and Jack's father came in from a night of drinking. The two police officers who arrived on the scene before the coroner seemed to think there were more bruises around the woman's cheeks and eyes than would have happened in a fall down the stairs. If she had been killed in the fall, it seemed to them, the blood would have stopped flowing and the bruising wouldn't have occurred. But perhaps because Jack's father knew one of the police officers on the scene—and the sergeant and the captain at the police station who were drinking buddies—no autopsy was performed. No investigation followed, and it was quickly deemed an accident and filed as such. Still, Jack had always wondered.

King John I said the grace and the food began its rounds, beginning with him, of course. It was all sort of medieval, the master of the house getting the best cut, then the next in the pecking order and so on down the line. Tina had learned that if she wanted to assure herself and little Maria of a meal, she had to make plenty of everything each time.

"That granddaughter of mine is the cutest thing," John Flynn said. "She's got my eyes."

"Maybe your temperament, too, Dad," Jack said, flashing a quick smile and holding it, hoping his father would latch onto it, too, which he did.

"Nah, I don't think so," he said, and for a moment he looked almost benevolent. "Well, maybe. She is pretty sweet." He laughed at his own joke and the rest of the family dutifully followed.

A light shone through the shades and Jack felt a chill run up his spine. The Back Bonnet Road wasn't all that well traveled, not like a city street might be. This was a rural town. Back Bonnet ran out past the old landfill to where the sand mines and slate quarries had been at different times in the town's history. One never saw Volvos or Mercedes out here; if anything, it was more likely to be dump trucks or pickups, and then only during the day. Any night traffic would be quite late, high school couples going parking or under-aged kids looking for a place to share a bottle of blackberry brandy.

Jack took a mouthful of stew and burned his mouth. He sucked in his breath. "Damn, that's hot!" he snapped, shooting an angry scowl at Tina. "Why didn't you tell us it was so damn hot?"

Tina averted her eyes and said quietly, almost under her breath, "Your dad said he liked the food hot. That's what he said last night."

Just for an instant, Jack's eyes and his father's locked and he shot his father a dagger of a look. But King John's gaze didn't flinch or drop, and the old man showed no fear. So Jack turned a withering gaze back onto his wife. She was looking down into her food, head bowed, shoulders slumped. She knew better than to give him an opening, any opening. Jack's anger smoldered with no place to ignite.

Headlights flashed across the window shade again, this time from the opposite direction.

"Who in hell is that out there going back and forth?" Jack snarled, standing up fast. The feet of his chair scraped the wooden floor, the chair nearly tipping over. He walked to the window, placed a finger inside the curtain, and pulled it aside slightly. It was black outside, almost total darkness save for a streetlight fifty yards down the street.

He was about to let go of the curtain when he saw the headlights returning. The old black hearse cruised by slowly. But when it passed under the streetlight he noticed it wasn't the familiar hearse. This one was very old and looked like a '59 Cadillac, the one that had the huge tail fins and looked like a Batmobile. Only this wasn't a Batmobile; it was clearly a hearse and older than 1959. Could this be something an 18 year-old motor-head had bought and custom-painted so he'd be the envy of his school friends? No doubt such an 18 year-old would sport tattoos like Jack's father and Jack had. For a moment he relaxed, his imaginings allowing him to identify with the car's owner.

"Who is it, Jack? Who is it, boy?" King John called from his chair at the end of the table.

"Oh, it's just some old beat-up hearse," Jack said.

"Looks like the Batmobile."

"The Batmobile?" his father said.

Jack heard something in his father's voice he'd never heard before. Fear.

"You sure it looks like a Batmobile?"

Jack glanced out the window again. The hearse sat parked under the streetlight, driver's door and passenger door both open. Two huge men in black suits and white shirts stood on the curb. Even at the distance Jack was certain they were wearing sunglasses and the stovepipe hats that reminded him of chimney sweeps.

"They look like Ackroyd and Belushi in *The Blues Brothers*," Jack said.

"Agh, damn!" his father cursed. "Damn it! Damn

it! Damn it! Is there a skull and a crossbones painted on the passenger door?"

Jack squinted. "There's something on there. Could be. Too far to tell, but it sure looks like it."

"Damn!" his father said again. "It's the banshee." Jack turned and gaped at his father. "What?" he said.

"The banshee."

"You mean, like in the movie *Darby O'Gill and the Little People*?" Jack said, the words tumbling out of his mouth now. "Where the phantom stagecoach of Death comes down from the sky to take Darby away because he's sold his soul and it's collection time?"

"Yes, basically," the old man said. "I don't know if it's someone surrendering his soul on collection day, as you put it, but it does mean someone here is going to die. The banshee has sent the hearse here for the soul."

Jack thought something in his father's voice sounded false. But he did recall his mother telling him about the banshee before she died.

John Flynn stood up from the table, walked to the gun cabinet in the corner, and withdrew a shotgun and a box of shells.

"Are they here for you, Dad?" Jack asked.

His father cracked the gun's double barrels and plugged a shell into each, emptying the remainder of the shells into his side pocket.

"Dad?" Jack asked.

"Grab yourself that shillelagh by the door, boy," the old man said, pointing to the gnarled wooden stick in the umbrella stand. When Jack didn't move quick enough, his father's voice grew nasty. "Grab it, boy. Grab it, I said."

Jack's hand closed on the twisted cane his father had used on his back and backside many times.

"Pick it up, boy," his father said. "We may need it."

Jack picked it up, hefted it in one hand, and

slapped it against his palm the way his father had done so often when threatening him. Doing it now sent a surge of adrenaline flowing in his system.

"We have to defend ourselves," his father said, and Jack, despite finding it hard to believe that the hearse was anything other than this-worldly, found himself nevertheless responding to his father's orders as if there was no question this was a hearse from hell and the two men the banshee's henchmen.

"Take the girl," the old man commanded Tina. "And get in the bedroom. Hunker down under the covers. We'll let you know when it's safe to come out."

Jack's wide-eyed wife scooped up the toddler in her arms and disappeared into the bedroom.

"Where are they now?" the old man said.

Jack peeked out. One man smoked a cigarette, the other stood looking at his watch. The kitchen clock said 6:29. The two men climbed back into the hearse and its headlights came on with a flicker. It rolled slowly toward the house.

"They're coming!" Jack said.

His father turned the recliner to face the door, sat in it, and drew a blanket up as if he was about to take a nap. He slid the shotgun under the blanket, aiming it at the door.

"Hang onto that shillelagh, son," he said. "This could be the fight of our lives." It was the first time Jack could remember him calling him son.

The hearse had pulled up in front. Its headlights went out and both men got out and walked toward the house.

"They're almost here, Dad."

"Wait for them to ring," the old man said. The old man clutched his chest and popped a nitro pill into his mouth.

The doorbell rang.

"Just a minute," Jack called, gripping the shillelagh so he could do some damage.

"Who is it?" Jack said.

No one answered.

"Who is it?" he said again, still not opening the door.

"We're here for John Flynn," said a voice from the other side.

"John Flynn?" Jack said. "He lives somewhere else. He moved."

"I don't think so, sir," said a deep voice from the other side. "This is 804 Back Bonnet. We're certain John Flynn has not moved. We have instructions to pick him up."

Jack's face went white. He looked at his father, whose face had also gone pale.

"You can't come in just now," Jack said, stepping back from the door in case they tried to kick it down.

Suddenly the two men were standing inside, though the door hadn't moved. They were right in front of Jack, as if he had blinked and they'd materialized.

"Who are you?" Jack said. "How'd you get in here?" He gripped tight the shillelagh.

Both men wore black gloves, so Jack couldn't see their hands. Their sunglasses were oversized and Jack couldn't see through them. Their hats were pulled down, their collars turned up. What little bit of facial flesh he could see looked more like tanned leather than human skin. The mouths moved weirdly as the men spoke their words.

"John Flynn," one of them said. "This is a pickup. 6:30 p.m. February 21."

"February 21 be damned," Jack yelled, brandishing the shillelagh like a cudgel. "You're not getting him!"

"Oh, we'll have him," the second man said. "We always do."

"But why?" Jack said. "What's this all about?"

The first man's lips moved woodenly. "We have orders to pick up John Flynn."

"And who do you represent?" Jack said. "Are you with a funeral parlor?"

The second man said in his deep voice, "You might say that."

The first man raised his voice, "Where is John Flynn? It's time."

Jack looked in terror toward his father and saw the blanket move by his knee. His father nodded and Jack backed away. The cover rose slightly and suddenly the shotgun roared. The blast made Jack's eyes squeeze shut, but when he opened them the two men were still there. A second blast pockmarked the door with holes. Cold air blew in through the shattered window, the flapping shade in shreds. The men were unscathed.

"John Flynn," the hearse driver said slowly and deliberately. "John Flynn."

The old man gasped for breath and clutched his chest, his face whiter than ever.

Jack swung the shillelagh with all his might. It cut through the men as if they were fog and struck the front door. The two men never flinched.

"Now!" boomed the voice of the second man. *"John Flynn! Now!"*

Jack backed closer to his father. "Are you all right, Dad?"

His father looked up weakly, eyelids half-closed with pain.

"Do you need another nitro, Dad?" Jack said.

His father nodded, and Jack grabbed the pillbox from the side table. He slid a pill under his father's tongue.

"Get the hell out of here!" Jack screamed at the ghouls standing over them. "You can't have him."

"John Flynn," the driver said firmly. "Now!"

Jack looked first at his father, then at the bedroom door where Tina and the children lay in hiding.

The men in black raised their right hands then and, for an instant, Jack saw them clearly—or was it his imagination? He was staring into the faces of two skeletons, two skulls under two hoods, two Grim Reapers. He began to cry and shake.

"*John Flynn!*" their voices boomed in unison.

Jack raised his own bony finger then and—for a moment, a fleeting moment—he had a heroic thought. *I'm John Flynn*, he would say, and his father would finally be proud of him. *I'm John Flynn. Take me.* But instead he gazed down at his father cowering in the recliner, this old man clutching his chest and wincing in pain, this old man who had beaten him so many times, dominating him all his life.

"Father, forgive me," Jack said. He made the sign of the cross with one hand and pointed to the bedroom door with the other. "In there's John Flynn. *He's in the crib!*"

# The Peanut Harvest

The peanut harvest was in full swing. That's what they called it at Alexandre's Ragtime Bar when Sunday morning came and Chucky, the dull-witted custodian, began sweeping up the peanut shells that littered the floor.

Steve, the manager/owner, was washing dishes and bar glasses that had been turned in after closing. The bartenders washed glasses only while they were serving drinks. The dirties that came in from the tables after the bartenders left, well, that was work that Steve had to do himself. It was only the two of them in the bar now, Steve and Chucky. Steve ran hot water in one of the two small bar sinks. He had the fans and smoke-eaters working, trying to clear out some of the smell from the night before. As was always the case on Sunday mornings, the place smelled like stale beer, peanut shells, and popcorn. Saturday was the only night he offered the free peanuts to patrons. He also had a live ragtime band, and surprisingly it attracted a fairly young crowd, one that normally would be drawn to rock music or heavy metal.

The place was always full, and by the end of the night the peanut shells were more than two inches deep. People slogged through them, so, mixed with the laughter, loud talk, and the ragtime band's brass and piano, there was a constant crunch-crunch-

crunch underfoot. The management—well, Steve—encouraged people to drop the empty peanut husks on the floor, something they'd have done anyway. Occasionally people—usually newcomers—stood and tried to dance, but the slippery peanut shells made it difficult. Ragtime Peanut Night was an idea whose time had come; it just worked, and people talked about it all over town. What started with a few pounds of peanuts now surpassed perhaps a million pounds—Steve didn't really know how many any more. He ordered huge garbage bags of them from a wholesaler.

"How goes the peanut harvest over there, Chucky?" Steve said.

Chucky looked up stupidly, said, "Good, boss. Peanut harvest goes good."

He'd already filled one garbage bag. Between the bar, the dining area, and the small dance floor, there were enough shells that it would take Chucky two hours to finish the cleanup. Afterward he'd wipe down the tables and chairs with sanitizing wipes.

Steve began cycling glasses through the two sinks, the first for wash, the second for rinse. He'd done a dozen glasses when he looked up and saw Chucky standing directly across the bar from him.

"Hey, boss. What's this?" Chucky said through thick lips, nodding at the dustpan in his hands. The pan was filled with peanut shells, and Steve only half-looked.

"It's the peanut harvest, Chucky. You know that. They're empty peanut shells. *Husks*, they call them."

"No. I mean *that*," he said, pointing at something close to the lip of the dustpan.

Steve looked more closely. It looked like a finger.

"Jesus," Steve said. "Hold it a little closer. Let me see that."

"Unh-unh!" Chucky grunted, shaking his head. "I ain't touching it."

"No. I mean, just move it a little closer," Steve said. "Let me see."

Sure enough, there in the dustpan was what looked like a finger, a long wrinkled white finger with dried blood at the end where it had met the palm. A flap of web-like skin to one side of the finger suggested it was either the index finger or the little finger. The ring and middle fingers would have skin flaps on either side.

"It looks like a finger to me," Chucky said, stating the obvious.

"It is a finger," Steve said.

"It's not mine," Chucky said, and he wiggled the fingers on his left hand, then set the dustpan down on the bar and wiggled the fingers on his right.

"I know that," Steve said. "There were no injury reports last night, none that I know of. I was on. We had three bartenders, five cocktail waitresses, and two bouncers, plus the band. No reports of an injury."

Chucky shrugged. "I just work mornings," he said. "What should we do with it?"

Steve grabbed a bar napkin, carefully picked up the finger, wrapped it in another bar napkin. "I'll call the crew, see if anybody knows anything about it. You go back to cleaning up."

Chucky took the dustpan, flipped the peanut husks into the trash bag, and began brooming the floor again.

Steve picked up the bar's little black phone book, called all three bartenders who'd been on. They didn't appreciate being awakened so early. None had anything out of the ordinary to report. He'd just hung up the phone when Chucky appeared in front of him again.

"Hey, boss. Look. Another one," Chucky said, holding up the dustpan.

There amidst the scattered peanut shells lay another finger, this one with a little webbing on both sides—either the middle or the ring finger, although there was no ring on it.

"Aw, Jesus God Almighty," Steve said. "What the hell happened here last night? Was there a mob hit or something? I'll have to call the police about this."

"You want to save this one, too?" Chucky said.

"Yeah, I think I better," Steve said. He wrapped the

second finger in a napkin, then dialed the police. He gave a quick explanation to the dispatcher, who promised a patrol car would be sent right over. He was tempted to stop what he was doing and to tell Chucky to stop as well, but there was still work to be done, and he had a noontime opening to get ready for. He busied himself washing glasses again.

"Hey, boss," Chucky called to him, standing with the broom in one hand, the dustpan in the other. "Come over here."

Steve grimaced. "Not another finger?" he said.

"No," Chucky said. "I think it's a thumb. Pretty sure."

Steve walked from behind the bar to where Chucky was working. There in the middle of a bare spot on the floor, where the peanut shells had been swept away, lay another pale, bloodless white digit—a right thumb. It looked almost like someone's big toe.

"I don't understand what's going on," Chucky said stupidly. "Are they falling off someone?"

Steve stared at the simpleminded janitor whose heavily hooded eyes looked so innocent.

"No, I don't think so, Chucky," he said. "I don't think they fell off. More likely they were cut off."

"Cut off?" the janitor said with a pained face. "God, that must have hurt."I'm sure it did," Steve said.

"But who cut them off?" Chucky said.

"I don't know," Steve said. "The police will be here in a couple of minutes to investigate."

"You think somebody got mad and cut somebody else's hand off?" Chucky said. "Or did the person cut their own fingers off?"

"I don't know," Steve said. "I don't know if it happened here."

"But the fingers are here," Chucky said.

"I know. But maybe the fingers were mixed in with

the peanuts when they arrived. Maybe it was the fingers of somebody who helped to pick the peanuts back in Georgia or wherever they come from—a farm hand." Steve regretted the word choice as soon as he said it. "Not literally a farm hand, Chucky, but a farm hand as in a worker, not really a hand."

Chucky giggled. It did seem kind of funny—farm hand.

"Well, what should we do?" Chucky said.

"I think we'll keep sweeping up, the two of us, until the police arrive. We'll just work very carefully, and we'll see if we find any more fingers. Sweep softly, Chucky, and let me know what you find. I'll get another broom and dustpan."

Steve had just started for the broom closet when Chucky called out, "I got another one, boss, and another one. Two right close together."

Sure enough, two more fingers lying on the floor.

"Just leave them there," Steve said. "Keep working. There's plenty more floor to sweep. That should be all five fingers from the hand."

"Five fingers?" Chucky asked, looking puzzled. "You mean four fingers and the thumb."

"Yes, four fingers and the thumb," Steve said, not bothering to argue. "I don't think we'll find anything else, but let's look carefully. I'll be back to help in a minute. I've got to unlock the front door for the policeman who's coming."

Now he wished he hadn't called the police, because he was sure it would be treated as a crime scene and he wouldn't be able to open. He'd lose business. And when the word got around that it was a crime scene—whether there'd actually been a crime there or not—it would get into the papers and hurt his business more. How much easier it would have been to sweep the fingers into a bag and dispose of them. But he knew he couldn't do that. Fingerprints needed to be taken, in case someone had been murdered or kidnapped. Families might need closure.

Steve pulled back the deadbolt from the front door, opened it, and took a quick look outside. No cops yet. He closed the door, leaving it unlocked.

"Hey, boss. Boss!" Chucky called out. "Here's three more! All thumbs."

Steve felt his breath draw in. "What? You're kidding, right, Chucky?"

"No, boss. I don't kid. Come here. Look."

Steve moved to the dance floor that lay buried in peanut shells. "Oh, Jesus," he said.

There, looking like three little long islands in the middle of a pond, lay three fresh thumbs in the sea of shells. The thumbs were perhaps twenty feet from the first thumb Chucky had found, and twenty-five to thirty feet from the various fingers. Judging from the attached webbed skin, these thumbs all looked like right thumbs. So now there were four right thumbs, meaning four victims.

Steve found himself wishing a group of his friends would jump from hiding and yell Surprise. But nobody did. It wasn't his birthday, wasn't close to his anniversary, but he could still wish it was a practical joke. It wasn't.

A knock sounded on the door, followed by "Police. Did you call?"

Steve yelled, "Yes. Come in."

Two officers walked in, glanced at the blanket of peanut shells covering the floor.

"Somebody had a party last night," one said with a smile. The other cop smiled, too.

"You found a finger while sweeping up?" the first officer said. "That right?"

"Lots of them," Chucky interjected before Steve

could answer. "Fingers and thumbs." Both cops squinted at Chucky then shot Steve one of those Is-he-all-there glances.

"It's true," Steve said. "Every time we sweep a little, we find more. We just found these three thumbs." He pointed down at the three narrow little islands that stood out on the floor. "There's another thumb over there, and some fingers just beyond it. And two fingers I wrapped in napkins on the bar."

"Any fights or injuries?" asked the second cop.

"Nope," Steve said. "I called my three bartenders who were on last night, and none of them had anything to report."

The cops stared down at the three thumbs.

"I'm praying these were in the peanuts when they arrived," Steve said.

"Not likely," said the cop who had made the crack about a party. "If the fingers and thumbs arrived with the peanuts, your tavern crowd would have reported it. I doubt they'd have fished one out of the peanut bowl, examined it, and thrown it on the floor. By the way they're widely scattered here, it's likely that more than one person would have discovered them, so keeping it quiet would require a conspiracy of silence."

"So what do you think then? Where did they come from?" Steve asked.

"Well," said the first cop. "That's a good question. All we can do is write this up. Right now I'm going to call in the homicide investigators. Consider this a crime scene until its declared otherwise. Just leave everything where it is. Don't do any more cleanup. We've got a few more questions to ask you on today's report."

The crime scene team uncovered more than a hundred and fifty fingers and thumbs that day. All the severed digits were fingerprinted, of course, and as many of the previous night's patrons as could be located were interviewed. None of them was missing any fingers or thumbs.

No satisfactory explanation was ever found. All the thumbs and fingers were found to be genuine human flesh. All had A Positive blood. Even odder, all the finger and thumbprints matched one another. All the thumbs were the same, all the fingers were the same— each index finger, each ring finger, each middle finger, each pinky had identical fingerprints.

The pathologist concluded the fingers and thumbs had not been cut off, but had fallen off—had been *sloughed* off, *shed* the way a snake's skin is sometimes left behind on the ground.

During the investigation only the thumbs and fingers that had been found on the floor were fingerprinted. None of the staff—Steve, Chucky, bartenders, bouncers, cocktail waitresses—was ever checked for fingerprints. They were simply examined to see if they had any fingers missing.

About three months after the incident, one of the cocktail waitresses quit. Had anyone thought to check, they'd have found she was A Positive and her fingerprints matched the sloughed-off fingers and thumbs. It saddened her to lose Alexandre's Ragtime Bar, because for almost a year the peanut harvest had offered the perfect incubation setup. The job allowed her to conceal the digits when she was in the shedding mode, and the peanut shells provided the rich compost the fingers and thumbs needed. New bodies could grow from them, and they too would shed their own digits and multiply. The peanut harvest had worked for several cycles, but ironically had been spoiled by a dimwitted janitor, the village idiot. In the coming months she'd have to risk another beer-and-peanuts bar on the West Coast or perhaps drive to

## Even Odder ✳ STEVE BURT

Georgia and hire on as a picker—better yet, a warehouse worker—at one of the huge peanut farms. Whichever she chose, she'd have to decide soon. In two months her hands would begin to grow heavy again, and shedding season would be upon her.

# Caretaker

It was one of the first signs of spring. Uncle Bowie was preparing to mow the graveyard.

The cemetery was an unusual one. There were more than a half dozen in town: the Catholic, the small Jewish cemetery, the Congregational cemetery behind the church, another behind the Baptist Church, and two all-purpose cemeteries. Then, of course, there was a pet cemetery, not in the scary Stephen King sense, but a place where people's dogs and cats or parrots were laid to rest—or their ashes, if cremation was the preferred method of disposing of a body—and stayed at rest.

But this one, the one Uncle Bowie took care of, was the Potter Cemetery, a unique and special cemetery set up by the State. There were only twelve graves in it. Those buried in Potter Cemetery, Uncle Bowie had always told me, were there because no one had claimed their bodies, and all the marvels of forensic science hadn't been able to identify them. They were classified, he said, as homeless people, drifters, hoboes, and various other terms. All were men, no women among them. Some had been found dead beneath underpasses or near railroad tracks at various locations around the state. One common link among them was that they had been persons no one, society or individuals, cared for or wanted. The other link was that many of them had died violent deaths.

The crimes cried out for justice and received none.

Uncle Bowie, now six months shy of ninety, had been tending Potter Cemetery since its inception in 1944. For his labors—mowing, pruning, filling in low spots, keeping the white picket fence around it painted every couple of years—he received the sum of four thousand dollars a year and the free use of a 1954 12' x 25' house trailer which he heated primarily with wood, with a kerosene stove backup. In 1944 he'd started at $200 a year and the free use of an old cabin, which was torn down when the trailer went up on the site. The State, in an arrangement with the Town, kept him in free firewood. A drilled well provided water, so all he had to pay was his electricity, food, and basic expenses. Because he didn't own the trailer, there were no property taxes. Uncle Bowie also worked odd jobs around town for the rest of his income until he was able to draw Social Security at sixty-five. For an 89 year-old man he was still in pretty good shape and could swing a hammer, handle a light axe or hatchet, and wrestle a mower around.

This year, however, he'd broken his foot in a fall on the ice a couple days after Valentine's Day, so he'd asked me to come help him with the first mowing or two. I'd just retired at 65 and had cashed my own first Social Security check, so I had time on my hands and thought this might be an opportunity to work into a partnership with Uncle Bowie. The cemetery job being part time and only six or seven months of the year, I could afford to pick up a small trailer for myself in Florida for the coldest months of the winter. In my head it seemed like quite a plan.

So, on a Friday night in mid March, I went to visit my uncle, carrying with me a pint of blackberry brandy, which I knew he appreciated. Not to say he was a drunkard, not by any means, but he did appreciate a nip or two a couple times a week, especially on cold winter nights. He wanted to give me an overview of the plans for mowing the next day.

"The mower's all gassed up, set to go," he said. "I cleaned it this week, gapped the spark plugs, sharpened the blade, greased the wheels, put fresh oil in the crankcase. It's in the shed, itching to go."

"And what about the pruning shears?" I said. "They oiled and sharpened, too?"

"Don't need those for awhile," Uncle Bowie said. "Won't be trimming the trees and bushes for another month."

"And how about a shovel or two so we can top off a couple of those graves that may have sunk during the winter?" I said.

"We'll do that next week," he said. "No need to worry about that now. Tomorrow we just do the first mowing."

I took a sip of my brandy. Something puzzled me, and it took me a minute to find words for it.

"Uncle Bowie, why are we mowing now?" I said. "It's only mid March. There won't be any grass for another six weeks, maybe eight."

"Because you've got to get this first mowing in now," he said. "Before it gets out of control."

I was pretty sure I'd misheard him, that he'd said "before it gets out of control."

"But Uncle Bowie," I said. "Grass—even weeds—won't be getting out of control for quite awhile."

"Well," he said, tipping back his shot glass and draining the rest of his brandy. "It's more of a mulching project, really. You know, sticks and branches, they come down over the winter. If you get them now, they're not a problem later."

"Then why don't we just take a couple of rakes," I said, "Now, before the grass comes in. Shouldn't be too hard to collect up all the twigs and branches, rake them into piles. We can either burn them or cart them away."

"Nope. Nope," he said abruptly. "That's not the way I do it, that's why. There's a certain way things have to be done here, and you've got to learn it. If you've got any idea of taking this over from me in the future—I hadn't said a word to him about this—you've got to learn to do it the right way. I know I can't do it much longer, and it's going to take a special person. Being the groundskeeper at Potter Cemetery isn't a job for just anyone."

I fought hard not to giggle. I didn't want to insult my uncle. In my head, something as simple as keeping a little one-acre cemetery in shape didn't seem like it required any special talent. But I didn't want to blow the prospect of a secure retirement for myself.

"Am I hearing you correct?" I said. "Are you proposing sort of an apprenticeship for me here this year?"

"Well, something like that," he said. "I think it'd be a good idea if you did learn it. But you've got to pay attention, and you've got to do it my way. Agreed?"

I agreed.

"Fine then. We'll see you tomorrow morning. Around 8:30. Come get me here at the trailer."

I downed the rest of my blackberry brandy, grabbed my hat, and said good night.

The next morning I looked out across the cemetery.

"Well, we caught them just in time," Uncle Bowie said.

I had no idea what he could mean. It looked to me as if there was plenty of time. As I had stated earlier, the grass wouldn't be up for quite awhile, and whatever mulching he was talking about could be done over the next month.

"It looks fine to me," I said.

"That's because you don't know what you're

looking for," Uncle Bowie said. "Let's go a little closer. But be careful where you walk here. Leave the mower where it sits."

I stepped from behind the big mower that had been designed for golf courses, a huge beast of a machine with handle grips like a motorcycle. The two of us moved to the very edge of the graveyard.

"Need to watch your footing here," Uncle Bowie said, "Or they'll grab you. You sure as heck don't want to trip and fall down around here." He pointed off to his right a couple of feet. There, sticking out of the ground, was a bony wrist and hand. No skin, just bones.

"What is it?" I said, knowing my uncle could hear the fear in my voice.

"It's exactly what it looks like," he said. "Just watch for a minute."

We stood over the skeleton hand, and I could feel my mouth hanging open. The thumb and fingers flexed—very slowly, to be sure, but they flexed. I gasped.

My uncle put his hand on my wrist and said softly, "Just wait. Watch."

A moment later the fingers tried to clench again, very slowly, then straightened out.

"What the hell's going on, Uncle Bowie?" I said. "Is this robotic? Battery-operated? Put here to scare somebody?"

"Ruger," he said, clutching a little tighter on my wrist. "This is no joke. Look over here." And he pointed to his left.

Another bony hand, small enough to be a child's, had broken through the soil as far as the back of the hand, but hadn't yet exposed the wrist. There was only the faintest movement in the fingers, nothing more than a twitch. Ten feet ahead of us I could see two large hands poking through the ground, one a left hand, one a right, about eighteen inches apart, both no more than bones, the skeleton of someone long dead. The fingers and thumbs were wiggling madly, as if being jolted every millisecond by electricity.

"That's why we've got to mulch now," Uncle Bowie said. "If you don't start now, when the ground first softens up, in the mud season, they get ahead of you. You've got to keep them down early. And like I said, God help you if you fall down."

I scanned the graveyard from where I stood and saw more skeletonized hands, fingers, and wrists poking through the sod. Uncle Bowie tapped me on the arm and pointed to a far corner of the cemetery.

"There's big fellow over there," he said. "By that tombstone with the greenish moss on it. He killed two little girls in 1956. He's a big strong bugger, and you'll want to mow over there at least once a week."

"But—" I started to say.

"But why doesn't the State do something about it?" Uncle Bowie said. "They tried. They lost two caretakers the first eight months. So they called me in, showed me what was going on, and I told them I'd take care of it. That's what I've been doing ever since—I been taking care of it. The State people who originally hired me for the job have long since died themselves, or retired and moved away. The point is, anyone with any memory of what really happens here is long gone. But the State keeps the checks coming, and the amount is so small for taking care of a tiny cemetery that even the biggest budget-cutters don't bother looking to give it the ax. And me? Well, you might think I don't raise the issue because I have a vested interest, thinking I've been feathering my nest all these years, which to some extent is true. But it's also true that there's a lot of accumulated evil here, and it wants to manifest itself in some ungodly way from beyond the grave. It's given me a sense of mission, of purpose. And that, as much as anything else, is why I do it."

"But what about the bodies of those calling out for justice—that story you told me so many times over the years?" I said.

"Well, it ain't true," Uncle Bowie said. "I said it because I needed a cover-up. Truth is, once you look at all those graves and markers, you'll find they're all between 1944 and the end of the death penalty. They're all full-grown men, with the exception of one midget there whose hands looks like a child's. And they all committed the most unspeakable crimes. It looks like only twelve, but that's because six aren't marked. I've got them all plotted out on a map in the trailer, so you can keep track. Each one was put to death by the State. Most of them were legally executed. A few, however, had unfortunate accidents at the Big House just after the death penalty was declared unconstitutional by the Supreme Court."

I was too stunned to speak, and my uncle saw that. He took advantage of the silence.

"This foot of mine—I told you it was a broken foot. That's close to the truth." He sat on a boulder and pulled up his pants leg. He took off his shoe and his sock. "This here's why I've been laid up," he said. "Four broken bones, one a compound fracture of the little toe, the other a compound fracture of the big toe. And over two hundred stitches." He rubbed his foot. "It's cold most of the time, too. Damaged the circulation. I was lucky to break free of him and get help before I could bleed to death."

He read the shock in my face. "That's right, Ruger," he said. "*It was him.*" He pointed an accusing finger out over the cemetery at the pair of huge hands. "*And them.*" He made a sweeping hand gesture that covered the whole graveyard. "I'm—I'm afraid I'm getting too old and weak to fight them off."

He looked me square in the eye, and I swallowed hard. I knew what was coming next.

"You wanted to take over when you thought it was just a cemetery to mow, Ruger, when you thought it was a cushy job. But what about now? Are you up to it, Ruger?"

I said nothing. My heart was pounding fast. I felt like he'd asked me to charge an enemy machine gun nest alone. He saw my fear.

"I'm sorry, nephew," he said. "I know I've placed you in an awkward position. And you don't have to say yes or no now. Think on it, Ruger. Think on it and let me know. If you say no, I'll try and find somebody else."

I nodded weakly. "I'll think on it, Uncle Bowie," I said. And I started to walk away.

"Wait a minute, nephew," he called out. "You can't leave just yet. We've got to get this first mowing in, and it's got to be today. I *need* you today, even if it's only for today. Help me today and then let me know tomorrow. That'll give me time to get somebody else."

Out of the corner of my eye I saw several bony fists clutching and releasing. The giant set of hands seemed to beckon me. My own hands trembled.

"Just this once," I said. "I'll help you out this once, Uncle Bowie, because of your foot. I doubt I'll say yes. In fact, I'm sure I'll say no. But I'll call and give you my answer in the morning."

"Thanks," Uncle Bowie said with a grin. "I appreciate it, Ruger. And don't be surprised if you find it's more fun than you thought."

I fired up the engine, engaged the deadly blade, and put the big mower in gear. For a brief moment, as I looked out over the twitching, clutching field before me, my heart was in my throat and I was afraid. But then, once I advanced upon the graveyard and heard the crack and crunch of bones and branches, the fear subsided and I felt a rush of adrenaline, the thrill of pure power.

"Chew them up good, Ruger," Uncle Bowie yelled to me from his perch on the boulder. "Chew up as many of those wretches as you can, son. Lay into them." He sounded insane, almost gleeful. "Don't forget, though, they come back up again and again, like the grass and the weeds—all fresh and new and nasty."

I turned the mower in the direction of the giant hands and took aim. The hands opened and closed like pincers as I bore down. I knew right then that I didn't need until morning to give Uncle Bowie his answer. I'd tell him when I finished the first mowing. I felt giddy. And to think they'd pay me to do it.

# VAMPIRE

Uncle Benrus always told us he was a vampire, but we never believed it. Well, we did—but we didn't; it was like that. It was those funny long, fang-like eyeteeth, those incisors that he had on the corners of each side of his mouth. They were longer than most people's. Everybody made fun of him when he was in school, I suppose, and made fun of him when he was an adult. He did look like Count Dracula, though, like that Bela Lugosi fellow, he really did. He had the dark hair and a gaunt face, but my God, it was those eyeteeth that really pegged him.

My cousin Harry and I asked our mothers about Uncle Benrus being a vampire. They were his younger sisters. They said that when they were growing up they'd never had any problems with losing blood. Oh sure, they'd wondered at times, too, because of his looks, and had even stayed up a few times to see if he'd sneak off in the night to hunt for victims. But he slept through the night like everybody else. Besides, they pointed out, Uncle Benrus was always out and around during the day, and everybody knows vampires can't go out then because of the sunlight—they shrivel up and turn to dust. So, reassured by what our mothers said, we went about our daily lives, never really thinking that he could be one. Well, no, we did think he *could* be one, but really didn't *believe* that he was. But what if he was?

When Harry and I were eleven—we were only three months apart—there was a murder across the tracks on the other side of town. It was a Puerto Rican woman who was known to party a lot. She wasn't married but spent time with different men. It was never specifically stated that anything funny was going on, but that was the impression we got.

One Sunday morning she didn't show up for church. She was found at home on her couch with two holes in the side of her neck—holes like you'd expect a vampire would leave when he drained a person of her blood or just took a little sip to keep himself going for awhile. Apparently—if it had been a vampire—the vampire had taken more than a sip, because the woman was dead. This was not a case of one regularly feeding off a person until she finally died, which might take days or weeks or months. No, this woman had no blood left in her, so it was a full gorging. At least, that's what we heard around school. The published reports in the local newspaper didn't say that; they simply said she'd been found dead and her throat had been slit. There was no mention of loss of blood. But when someone's throat was slit, you could imagine there'd be lots of blood on the floor, or on the couch. The article wasn't clear on this.

But the kids at school, being teenagers—friends of ours supposedly, but not necessarily real true friends—began talking about our Uncle Benrus. They suggested it might have been him who committed the crime. They'd seen him many times. He'd taken us to school when our mothers had to work.

He was disabled—allergies or something—so he got a government disability pension from an old job he had at the Animal Disease Research Laboratory. He'd worked there for a year before they discovered the allergies, so they had to let him go and pay disability until he could find another job in the same field—which, of course, with the allergies, was impossible. He was, by the government's standards, disabled for life.

But that gave Uncle Benrus time to do what he loved, writing and publishing horror stories. One prize-winning story he published was about a vampire. Funny thing is, it was told in the first person, from the vampire's point of view. It was not only frightening; it was also heart rending. You really felt for the vampire, as with Anne Rice's *Vampire LeStat* and some of her other vampires. Harry and I read the story over a number of times. It seemed to us that it was an actual account that our uncle had written, a first-person account, and not a piece of fiction. So, despite what our mothers said about him not being a vampire, and even though we couldn't *rationally* believe it was true, the two of us were convinced that Uncle Benrus was indeed a vampire, and that his stories, at least some of them, were true. So, as I said, to us—he was, and he wasn't.

The police showed up three days after the Puerto Rican woman was found dead. They didn't say that any puncture wounds had been found on the neck, nor did they indicate any evidence of vampirism; they simply wanted to talk to our uncle because they had heard rumblings around town, probably started by the kids at our school, or perhaps by the adults.

Uncle Benrus spent the better part of two hours with them. Neither Harry nor I were allowed in the room, but my mother and aunt were. We stayed outside the door, trying to see and hear through the keyhole. But we didn't hear much. If the questioning was tense, we wouldn't have known it because, occasionally, we heard laughter—our uncle and mothers and the police, as if they were all laughing at the ridiculousness of the notion there were real vampires in our world.

Harry and I were conflicted even though we knew this had nothing to do with a vampire. We were conflicted because—what if it was? We had our loyalty to our uncle, but at the same time we had our duty to the law. If someone had lost her life at the hands of our uncle, much as we loved him, much as he loved us—well, it places a strain on one's loyalties.

Six months after the Puerto Rican woman was murdered, a black woman in her late twenties was found dead three blocks from the Puerto Rican woman's house. This woman did not possess the reputation with men the first woman had. She was single—divorced, actually—and lived by herself. She too was found lying on her couch with her throat slit and blood pooled on the couch. She was found Sunday morning when she didn't show up for church. But her church was not the same as the Puerto Rican woman's.

At school we played armchair detective for days. It was our main topic of conversation. Could it be a churchgoer they knew in common, a third person who church-shopped? Could it be a minister who had dealings with both churches and both women? Had they both dated the same person? Were the police following up on these possibilities?

Of course, as with the first murder, speculation took over. Like the Puerto Rican woman, *the black woman could have been killed by a vampire.* This, the kids said, was why the news story had reported it as a slit throat rather than puncture wounds and blood sucked out—it was a vampirism cover-up—so the public wouldn't panic. Adults trotted that theory around the bars as well.

As before, the police arrived to speak with Uncle Benrus. This time it only took about forty-five minutes. It was the same two officers. We heard no laughter, but we did hear my uncle say at one point,

"My God, it's just a terrible thing, a terrible thing."

Harry and I tried to talk about it over supper. But our mothers, while they allowed us to talk about both murders, quickly dismissed any vampire talk as nonsense.

"The reason they came here to talk to your uncle was because the same silly vampire talk was traveling the streets," my mother said. "The officers assured us that there were no puncture wounds and no blood drained from the body—except what drains normally from a person whose throat has been slit. Yes, it was a grisly sight. Yes, they're sure it was murder. No, your Uncle Benrus is not a suspect. That's why they came by, as a courtesy, to let him know he wasn't under suspicion."

Harry, who had been reading a lot of Sherlock Holmes, said, "Yes, but even if it's not a vampire who perpetrated these hideous crimes, we still have a murderer on the loose. Two people murdered, six months apart. No clear suspect. The game's afoot."

"No, the game *is not* afoot," Uncle Benrus said firmly. "It is *not* a game and you two are not detectives. The police handle these matters. Don't get any ideas about playing Hardy Boys or Holmes and Watson." It was as sharply as our uncle had ever spoken to us. It was a silent supper after that.

Six months after the second murder, almost a year to the day after the first, another woman's body was found, also lying on her couch. She was four blocks from the first victim, six blocks from the second victim, a fact that Harry noted on a map of the town he'd tacked on our bedroom wall. He pin-marked the locations of all three murders, drew a triangle connecting the three, and circumscribed three different circles, one from each of the murder sites, creating a symbol like the interlocking Olympic rings. And he had the clippings from the three newspapers in an organized file system.

This third woman had been thirty, Caucasian, and lived with her father. She worked as a barmaid at a bar the other two women had visited at different times. Her father was not home at the time of the murder, he'd been on the West Coast visiting family. While that established his alibi, it also left him feeling terribly guilty that he hadn't been there to help his daughter. Her throat, too, had been slit, the newspapers said. And, as before, the speculation around town was that the slit throat was a vampire's cover-up to hide any puncture marks.

Had no one thought, Harry said, to try to measure the amount of blood that was found, to calculate if it was the amount that had escaped the body? If the body had X number of pints of blood, for example, and the blood that escaped onto the couch accounted for a third of that, and two thirds of it was still in the body, then all the blood was accounted for.

"But," he said, "What if only half the blood was accounted for, between what was on the couch and what was in the body? Where would the rest of the blood have gone?"

"That's an excellent question," our uncle's voice said from behind us. "I'm sure the police have thought of that. A coroner's job is to take such measurements of all bodily fluids and to carefully note the site of the wound. A coroner is a medical doctor—trained for autopsies, by the way—and would know if a puncture wound were being concealed under a slitting wound."

Uncle Benrus stared hard at us, delivering the words slowly, making his point to be sure we heard and thought about every word—every *warning*. Yes, *warning* was the word that came to me. As I looked up at his hard stare, it seemed to me his eyes had a slight redness to them, like the red glare you get in flash photographs of certain people.

"But Uncle—" Harry started to say, and Uncle Benrus raised his finger to shush us.

"You are *not* detectives," he said again, slowly, deliberately, forcefully. "Stay out of it. Your mothers have enough to worry about without fretting over your safety. Understood?"

We nodded and our uncle left the room.

That night, after we climbed into our bunk beds and turned out the lights, Harry said to me, "Did you notice anything funny about Uncle Benrus's eyes today when he talked to us?"

"What do you mean?" I said.

"I mean, like he's been a lot edgier lately, not as easygoing. When he gets tense—I mean, he's fine when he's laughing and having a good time, but when he gets tense—well, I thought I saw his eyes flash red today when he was warning us off."

I held my breath, didn't know what to say.

"Well?" Harry said. "Did you notice it or not? Or was it my imagination?"

"I saw," I said.

"So what do you think?" Harry asked.

"I think," I said, pausing to make sure I worded it as carefully as I could, "I think our imaginations are getting the better of us. I think many people's eyes show red or pink. Like when you shoot pictures indoors and the flash reflects back on the film, the centers of the eyes look red. That's all."

"Not just red," Harry said. "*Demonic.* Don't you think?"

"I suppose," I said in the dark.

"You know who else has red eyes?" Harry said.

"No. Who?" I said.

"Vampire bats," he answered.

I sucked in my breath again. My heart jumped. An image of a bat's tiny face appeared in my mind, its fangs protruding like my uncle's eyeteeth.

"That's not funny," I said. "That's not funny at all."

"I know," Harry said. "I didn't mean it to be funny. It's scary, isn't it?"

I reached over and snapped on the light, climbed out of bed, and looked up at Harry on the top bunk. For a second I thought his eyes looked pinkish. But when I blinked, it was regular old Harry.

"Where you going?" he said.

"Bathroom."

A minute later I stood at the sink washing my hands. In the mirror my cheeks looked flushed. I felt hot and wondered if I had a fever. I ran water on a washcloth and held it over my face. The cool water felt wonderful.

"A little case of the night sweats?" Harry's voice asked from behind me.

I pulled the washcloth from my face and turned to look at him leaning against the door frame.

"Must be coming down with something," I said. "Hope it's not the flu."

"Upset stomach, vomiting, diarrhea?" Uncle Benrus said, suddenly appearing behind Harry.

"You okay, sweetie?" my mother said, standing beside Uncle Benrus, my aunt behind her.

"Everybody can go back to bed," I said. "I was just feeling hot, that's all."

"Is that from a nosebleed?" Mom asked, pointing at the washcloth in my hands.

On the damp cloth I saw bright red streaks. I checked the mirror. No sign of blood from my nostrils, but I felt pain in my gums and opened my mouth. The gum tissue around my eyeteeth was crimson, and the eyeteeth themselves had grown longer by half an inch.

I gaped at myself in horror, and for a second I felt a flash of anger. With that flash my eyes glowed pink.

"You'll need to learn to keep your emotions in check, boys," Uncle Benrus said. "Otherwise your eyes will give you away."

"I'm about four hours ahead of you," Harry said, shrugging. "So it's all pretty new to me, too." He smiled and I saw that his eyeteeth were already twice the length of mine. "The fever passes fast," he said. "And Uncle Benrus says the fangs will be fully developed in a couple of days."

My mother and my aunt stood smiling as if watching a toddler take his first steps. They hugged me. Uncle Benrus shook my hand.

"There'll be plenty to talk about in the morning, boys," he said with a kindly smile and a wink. "Our version of the Birds and the Bees, if you know what I mean. So hold your questions for breakfast—including the one about why you can see your own reflections in the mirror. Trust me. Everything is as it should be. From now on, your lives will become both richer and more difficult. But you have much to learn. Welcome to the adult world."

# The Lobsterman

When Freddy Herman died with no next of kin, the Town Justice, who was also the Harbormaster's brother, called and asked me if I'd pull Freddy's lobster pots out of Long Island Sound. I did a little lobstering myself and now that Freddy was gone, there was no sense leaving his pots set without anybody to collect lobsters from them.

Freddy had been a heavy-drinker who lived in a tarpaper shack, heated his house with wood, and cooked on a little gas stove that ran off a propane tank outside his kitchen window. He played poker here and there around town. When he wasn't lobstering he might be scalloping or possibly opening scallops at somebody else's scallop shop to make a few bucks for booze and cigarettes. He never married, couldn't seem to hold a relationship and didn't seem interested in one. Now, at 66, he'd died.

I attended the funeral not because I'd known Freddy well, but because he'd been a bayman and there was a bond among those of us who made our living off the water—from scallops, oysters, lobsters, and various types of fish.

There were fifteen or twenty other full- and part-time baymen at the funeral. After the minister said a few words, he asked if anyone wanted to speak. A couple of people stood up and said what a good guy

Freddy was, a decent poker buddy, a man who could tell a good joke or a story. Two of them had gone to school with him up to the eighth grade before he dropped out. But the theme I heard, the one repeated by the half dozen people who spoke, was that Freddy had a knack for getting the largest lobsters and always bringing in his limit, no matter what day of the week or season. Someone joked that not all of Freddy's lobstering was in-season, and everybody laughed. When the few speakers had each said their piece, the minister offered a prayer then gave a benediction. Everybody stood up and started handshaking and chatting as if it was time for the Passing of the Peace at church. Then they moved into the next room for coffee and donuts. The whole funeral took less than fifteen minutes.

The body was cremated and the minister suggested it might be appropriate for other baymen to sprinkle the ashes at sea. No one volunteered. But when the question came up about Freddy's lobster traps still sitting on the bottom of the Sound, the group of not-really-grieving baymen learned that I'd been hired to pick them up. Someone suggested I sprinkle a few ashes with each pot I picked up. Harry Caymon, one of Freddy's gambling buddies and a longtime lobsterman, clapped a big hand on my shoulder and said, "All in favor, say aye," and everyone in the room said aye, of course, except I. That's how I was hired to retrieve Freddy's lobster pots and how I was elected to distribute his ashes.

It was a late Monday afternoon when I finally got out on the Sound. My plan wasn't to pull all of them then. I went out with my boat empty, figuring I'd haul up a few pots, tossing the lobsters back in as I went. I'd stack the slatted traps on board so I could deliver them to the Harbormaster. Freddy's estate was to pay me for my time at twenty dollars an hour, so why hurry? The next trip I'd pick up more traps and then some more. I knew how many traps he was legally allowed to lay down, but I didn't know how many he actually had.

As I approached the first one, I thought about all the stories I'd heard—not only at the funeral, but over the years—about Freddy always catching his limit and always catching big lobsters. I wondered what kind of chum he used to bait his traps—probably fish heads, like I did.

I reached the first buoy—each bayman's buoys are marked with a different pattern of colors—and hooked it with my gaff. I looped the rope around my power winch, engaged the clutch, and the wound the rope onto the spool, pulling the rectangular lobster trap up from the bottom of Long Island Sound.

Freddy's trap cleared the water with a splash. I swung it onto the culling board. In the trap wriggled three large greenish-brown lobsters. I opened the trap's door, extracted the lobsters, and tossed them back over the side.

What the others had said was true. Freddy did have a knack for pulling large lobsters. I looked closer to see what he'd been using for bait. I gasped. There, where a fish head or other piece of chum would normally be attached, hung the head of a cat, its dull lifeless eyes staring straight ahead. Its fur was soaking wet and slimy as a newborn kitten's. Where the head had been severed from the neck—I was quite sure that's what had happened—the flesh was jagged, and whatever had been the meaty part under the hide had been eaten away by small fish or other denizens of the deep. This left the skin beneath the fur looking more like a tanned hide. I was horrified. Had the cat already been dead when Freddy cut its head off? I couldn't stand the thought of bringing it back to shore, so I dropped the pot back over the side. It had to be something he was experimenting with. I'd pick up the next few pots instead.

Not fifty yards away I spotted familiar markings and pulled Freddy's second trap. It was jammed with large lobsters. But before swinging it onto the culling board, I checked his bait.

"Damn!" I said. "Freddy, you sick son-of-a-B."

There hung another cat's head. I dropped that pot back, too, without removing the lobsters, and moved on to the third pot. A third cat's head. I dumped the pot and turned for home.

The Harbormaster and the Town Justice were aghast. They said they understood why I was backing out of the contract. The Harbormaster apologized for saying something about getting "somebody with a stronger stomach to take care of it." He hadn't meant for me to take it personally.

Two days later the Justice called me in. He had located a distant cousin of Freddy's in California, a man who had exchanged Christmas cards with Freddy every year. When the cousin learned of Freddy's death, he phoned to say he wanted nothing to do with the estate; he didn't need rags or junk furniture. He asked if the Justice could appoint an executor to inventory and dispose of the belongings and property, then send the proceeds.

The Justice mentioned the cat heads.

Twenty years earlier, the cousin said, Freddy had written him a Christmas card saying he'd discovered cat heads made the best lobster trap chum. He wrote that he was coming out of a bar one night when he came across a cat crushed by a pickup truck. Since it was dead anyway, he took it home, removed its head, and tried it for bait. The cat's head was not only a hit; it lasted ten times longer than fish heads.

"The cousin thought it was all a joke," the Town Justice said. "He thought it was a story Freddy made up and then perpetuated through their Christmas card correspondence from year to year. He said he disposed of cats for local veterinarians and for the Pound for free. Apparently he became a one-man, Dead-Cat Cleanup Society."

If I hadn't seen the heads myself, I wouldn't have believed what the Justice was saying.

The phone rang in the outside office then, and MaryAnn the receptionist knocked and entered.

"Mrs. Collins is on the phone," she said. "She's inventorying Freddy's estate. She says you'd better send Animal Control over. There are dozens of animals in the cellar. It's a kitten factory."

"Tell her we'll get somebody there soon," the Justice said.

"Very well." And as the receptionist was closing the door she added, "She said she'll give them whatever milk and food she can find." The door clicked shut.

The Justice sat back, let out a sigh, and looked vacantly at me for a second. Then he jumped to his feet. "MaryAnn, wait!" he yelled, and I knew what he was thinking.

"Faster if you cut through the back yard," I said, pointing out the open window at the street behind Town Hall. "Freddy's is right there."

Too late. We heard a scream from the distance and a moment later saw Mrs. Collins sprint from Freddy's front porch. She leaped in her car, fired up the engine, and squealed her tires halfway down the street.

When the Justice and I got to Freddy's, we found Mrs. Collins's upchucked lunch on the floor in front of the refrigerator.

# The Spoon-Bender

My sister Anna was a spoon-bender. She also demonstrated some degree of clairvoyance. These gifts—if they can be called that, for I believe they ended up being her undoing—manifested themselves from the time she was eight until her untimely death at seventeen.

Anna was three years older than I and until she was eight she ran and played like any other child, attending school and church and family gatherings. She loved the outdoors. That's where we were—in a cow pasture with a single tree in the middle—when she was partially struck by lightning. I say *partially* because she wasn't struck directly, not so electricity shot down through her body and out through the feet. This was a glancing blow.

When the rain began, she grabbed my hand and led me under the tree, where she sat on top of a thick, partially exposed root with me on her lap. We cowered there while thunder boomed and lightning snaked across the skies, Anna's jacket pulled over our heads like an umbrella. Just when it appeared the storm was over, a single lighting bolt struck the tree, pitching me off my sister's lap like I was on a trampoline. I landed twenty yards away, and when I sat up I saw Anna on her side, face away from me. I was certain she'd been killed and I began to whimper.

Then I saw a slight movement and crawled toward her. She sat up, still facing away from me, and called out, "Pudge? Pudge? Where are you, Pudge?" I opened my mouth to say something when—*still facing away, before turning*—she said, "Oh, there you are, Pudge, behind me. Thank God you're all right." She turned then, her face white as a ghost, and drew me into her arms. I sobbed for five minutes.

Once things had quieted down we examined ourselves. I was muddy but had no injuries. Anna was unhurt but not untouched. The seat of her jeans and the soles of her shoes showed singe marks. The pupil of her left eye was completely dilated, a fact I noticed then and she later verified in a mirror at home. Despite dozens of visits to optometrists and ophthalmologists, neither the cause nor a corrective was ever found.

After that Anna was different, not so much psychologically or emotionally as—well, she would do stuff. Like bending spoons, for example, and forks, and nails, and coat hangers. Not with her hands, but without touching them.

And she could pick up pens. She'd hold her hand over a pen—three or four inches above it—and it would rise to meet her. I figured it was magnetism at first, but after awhile she developed the skills to lift a pen from across the room. Apparently she wasn't a magnet; everything didn't stick to her. She'd concentrate and—*thwup*, the pen would jump at her. But the table under the pen, even a metal table—we also tried metal trays—wouldn't move. And none of the other objects next to the pen—paper clips, coins, bottle caps—would move unless she willed them to move. The lightning strike had given her a very powerful mind.

This happened around the same time E.S.P. experiments became the rage at universities like Stanford. On

U.S. television Uri Geller, the Israeli mentalist and medium, was a phenomenon with his spoon-bending demonstrations. After one of Geller's demonstrations in Japan, my father said, it was reported that thousands of Japanese children were found capable of the same thing. Similar reports came in from Britain. I wondered if my sister's abilities weren't fairly commonplace.

Still, Anna told no one except me and our parents, which may as well have meant me alone. The first time she demonstrated spoon-bending for them, a few months after the lightning strike, my father (who had just finished reading about Uri Geller and the Japanese children) shook his head dismissively and said, "A day late and a dollar short, sweetie. Everybody's doing it." He either felt the "Geller phenomenon" was old hat or spoon-bending was a parlor trick my sister's class had learned in school.

I think our mother wanted to be more supportive but didn't want Anna to become a lab experiment. Mom no doubt counseled her about it, because I remember Anna saying more than once, "I don't want to be pinned down like a butterfly in a collection." Whatever the case, after one or two of Anna's demonstrations, the subject was dropped. But my sister practiced and developed her gift secretly.

Once, in her seventh-grade English class, I heard, the wastebasket by the teacher's desk shot into the air and flipped upside-down as the teacher was speaking. It happened so fast that it trapped all the trash against the tile floor; not one sheet of paper or crumpled gum wrapper escaped. The teacher yelled "Fire Drill", evacuated the class, and the wastebasket was checked for wires and springs. Nothing was found. The school was buzzing. That night when I asked her about it, Anna said, "It was a harmless prank, a joke."

Another time, when the two of us were in the same

classroom for a Latin exam—I was a sophomore, she was a senior, both taking Latin II—the clock on the wall said 2:05. The exam would end at 2:10, and my anxiety was rising. Not enough time. About three minutes later I looked at the clock again and saw that it was 2:03, not 2:08. I glanced at Anna, who winked and went back to her exam. The clocks in the entire school had jumped back five minutes, and the dismissal bell rang late.

I once asked her why, instead of turning over waste baskets and setting back clocks, she didn't develop her powers for—well, for Good, with a capital G, maybe become a superhero like Magneto. She said, "How do you know I haven't been? How do you know I'm not out at night while you're asleep, patrolling the streets of the city like Batman, Superman, and the Flash?" Then, with a mock sneer and the lift of an eyebrow she said, "Then again, how do you know I'm not Lex Luthor, Professor Moriarty, or one of the arch-villains?"

The thought had crossed my mind—not whether she might use her power for Evil, but perhaps for a Little Less Than Good. Certain instances made me wonder. Sometimes when she was with me at candy machines—before I put my coins in and pulled the levers—the candy would simply drop down. She'd get us M&M's, Clark Bars, Hershey Bars, whatever we wanted. One time candy bars and bags of salted peanuts rained down from the machine faster than I could remove them; the machine was empty in seconds. I wondered if she could do it with bank vaults, make the tumblers click in proper sequence and command the big doors to open by themselves, the way they did it on *Mission Impossible*. Whiz, click, whizzz, click, whizzzzzz, click. Clunk, whang, voila!

One might imagine my sister was a loner. She wasn't; she was a normal teenager. She had friends, loved to dance, was a majorette and twirled baton. No one had ever seen such a young person twirl so expertly. It appeared as if the baton spun without touching her fingertips. And she was the only majorette who never— *not ever*—dropped a baton.

The closest I ever saw her come to the superhero role was when we were walking home from school. A crowd had gathered around two of the high school's most notorious hoods who were busy wailing on each other with their fists. When the smaller one sensed he was losing, he stepped back as if to shuck his leather jacket, but instead whipped out a switchblade.

"Now let's see who's the big man," he snarled, slicing the air as he advanced.

Suddenly with all eyes on the shiny razor-sharp knife, the blade wilted. Like a dead flower, like cooked spaghetti, the knife went limp. And then as everyone stared slack-jawed, the blade simply melted and dropped to the ground the way a scoop of ice cream falls from a toddler's cone. Plop. When one of the hoods began to laugh, and then the other, everyone in the crowd joined in. Before long, people were holding their sides as tears of laughter streamed down their cheeks. The only one not laughing was Anna; she simply smiled curiously like the Mona Lisa.

Breaking up that fight could have been a turning point, a claiming of her superhero gifts. But it wasn't; she didn't go the Wonder Woman route. Instead, the more adept she became with her gifts, the more risks she took.

At seventeen she and I babysat our two cousins who lived in an upscale section of Massapequa Park, Long Island. Their family's house was lovely, with a pool in back and plenty of expensive furnishings and antiques throughout the house. Until that time, I had thought Anna's only gift was spoon-bending.

Around eight-thirty my two cousins and I were watching TV. Anna was sitting in the recliner in the lotus position, eyes closed and palms up as if meditating. Just as I glanced at her, her eyes flew open, her lips curled into a devilish smile, and she said in an excited whisper, "They're coming."

"Already?" one of my cousins said. "They said they'd be late."

"Not your parents," Anna said. "The burglars." Then, seeing the children's eyes go wide, she said cheerfully, "But don't worry. We'll have some fun. How about it, you three, want to have some fun?"

Anna told us the burglars would arrive at ten-fifteen, so we'd have to shut off the lights before ten and hide. There would be two of them, she said, and they'd be searching for jewelry, cash, and the wall safe behind the painting in the study.

"Here's what we need to do to get ready," she said. "First pull out all the pots and pans and line them up on the stove and the counter. Put lids on them. And be sure to put the blender, the toaster, the food processor, and a couple of radios on the kitchen table and on the counter. Set the radios on different stations and turn them up as loud as they'll go, but don't turn them on. *And don't plug anything in.* Oh, and make sure to lay all the silverware and utensils out on the counters, tables, on the fridge, wherever you can."

Once we'd done what she asked, she showed us where to hide.

"Whatever you see, whatever you hear, no matter how scary, don't move and don't cry out," Anna said. "Just stay put. It'll be over in about three minutes. Just enjoy it. Trust me." Never once did she say anything about calling the police.

At 9:45 everything was in place, all the house lights were out, and we took to our hiding places. We crouched quietly for twenty minutes, and my cousin Sid whispered loudly, "If there are burglars coming, where are they?"

"Ten-fifteen, Sid!" Anna said. "Ten more minutes. Now shush! They'll be here."

At ten-fifteen we heard a noise—the patio door. Someone was jimmying the lock on the sliding glass doors! In less than a minute we heard it slide open and felt a cool breeze from outside. We hunkered down, drawing blankets around our shoulders.

Voices whispered in the dark living room.

"You take the bedrooms," one said. "I'll check for the safe down here."

"First let's check the freezer for jewelry," the other said. "A lot of people hide their diamonds in ice."

We heard footsteps padding toward the kitchen.

"What if they look in here?" my cousin Sid whispered in my ear.

Before I could answer, all hell broke loose. The radios blasted at full volume, all on different stations. The living room TV turned itself on, zipping from one channel to the next in rapid succession. The blender and two electric mixers whirred and an egg timer dinged again and again. The microwave timer signaled over and over that that dinner was ready, and the four-barrel toaster popped up and down frantically. Every light in the house flashed on and off.

"What the hell?" I think one of the men called out over the confusion, and the two of them headed for the back door, looking like the herky-jerky actors in a flickering silent movie. One burglar placed his hand on the door knob and, as he did, the lids on the pots and pans clashed like a hundred crashing cymbals, adding to the insanity. The two rooms had gone mad.

"Let's get out of here!" the man at the door yelled, but the knob came off in his hand and before he could react, silverware and utensils flew around the kitchen like angry hornets. Blinded by the flashing lights, confused by crazy music and clanking pots, now ducking a barrage of cutlery, the men dove for the living room.

"The patio door!" a voice said, but it didn't sound like one of the men's. It sounded more like an impression of a man's voice; it sounded like Anna.

The burglars bought it. They covered their heads and ran for the slider. As they made their escape a torrent of knives, forks, spoons, and ladles clinked and clanged against the thick glass beside them. They stumbled through the open door and tumbled—splash—right into the pool.

Inside, even though one sliding door was open and the other closed, the silverware continued its noisy rat-a-tat assault on the door; but now it was mostly for effect, to let the burglars know it wasn't safe to re-enter the house. Whatever force had defended the house against their first intrusion, it was ready to assault them again. They climbed out of the pool and slunk away.

Five minutes later everything was quiet and the four of us crept from our hiding places. The silverware, cutlery, and electrical gadgets were exactly where we had placed them before the assault. The only thing different was the patio door. It was still open, wet tracks leading from the pool to the border bushes. Anna swore us all to secrecy, then had us put everything away.

The only moment of suspicion passed quickly when my aunt asked, "Did the electricity go off? The microwave, the answering machine, and the alarm clocks are blinking and need to be reset."

We four shrugged.

The year my sister got her senior driver's license was the year her power was its most developed. We drove to K-Mart to get something before the store closed. When we got there, there were only a few cars in the huge parking lot. But everywhere we looked were shopping carts, abandoned where shoppers had unloaded them.

Anna got out and stood beside one of those cart corrals made of iron pipes. She raised her hands the way the Pope did when he blessed the masses from his balcony, then made a slow sweep of her arms. It looked creepy, Dracula-like, as if she were a huge bird spreading its wings. Slowly and deliberately she took a deep breath and drew her arms across her chest in an X, right hand on left shoulder, left hand on right shoulder, a mummy position.

I sensed movement with my peripheral vision. The shopping carts were moving—first one, then several, then half of them, then all of them—slowly at first, then gaining speed, then all stampeding across the pavement toward the cart corral. Before they could crash into it, though, the carts aligned and neatly racked themselves one inside another until the trains were six and seven long.

"Now let's get what we came for, Pudge," Anna said, motioning me to follow her into the store. In less than three minutes she had called in every errant shopping cart in the huge lot. With a smirk she said, "Didn't want you to think I couldn't do a good deed once in awhile."

The "good deed" remark stuck in my head. Barely a week after K-Mart we went for a walk at a small lake not far from our house. An aluminum rowboat was tied to the end of a short dock. We sat on the edge of the dock, our feet hanging down in the water. Without a breath of wind the rowboat began to drift away from the dock. The rope grew taut and the boat strained to break free. I stared at the wood piling and the double-looped and knotted line securing the boat. *It began to untie itself.* It didn't just pull loose— the rope actually untied itself. The boat drifted toward the center of the lake.

"Did you do that, Anna?" I said.

Her eyes were closed and she looked totally relaxed. She didn't answer.

The boat stopped, made three revolutions clockwise, three counterclockwise. Anna was playing.

"Why are you doing that?" I said.

That queer little Mona Lisa smile came across her lips.

Suddenly I heard popping—like distant gunshots—coming from the rowboat. It looked like fireworks shooting out of it. The aluminum rivets holding the boat together were blowing out. Tiny fountains of water spurted into the air. In two minutes the boat had disappeared beneath the surface and lay on the lake bottom.

"That boat wasn't yours," I said.

But my sister was already on her feet and heading for dry land. It was beyond me to say anything more, but one thing I did know. She was gaining strength and confidence in her powers. And she was getting cocky.

Six months Anna was dead. I don't recall much happening between the rowboat incident and her death; I'm mostly blank there. But I do remember a conversation at the supper table—my sister and father getting into an argument. He said something like, "Next you'll be talking about astral projection and near-death experiences."

Anna said in her best know-it-all voice, "Oh, you mean the light at the end of the tunnel?"

I thought my father would say, "Yeah, yeah, like seeing the light at the end of the tunnel, *that kind of crap.*" But he didn't. Instead he said coldly, "You know, Miss Smart-Ass, sometimes the light at the end of the tunnel is a train coming at you." That ended the argument.

A few days later I was in school. Anna wasn't, even though we had ridden in together. I saw her name on the absentee list along with her two best friends' names. The two friends later told us what happened.

At Anna's insistence the three of them went to the railroad tunnel that ran under the highway. Despite her friends' pleading, Anna walked into it muttering something about "the light at the end of the tunnel" and "Do you believe a person can stop a train with their mind?" She went a hundred feet and squared off in the middle of the track. Both girls swore the train cut its speed in half before it reached the spot, though the engineer said he never saw her and didn't slow at all. Next thing they knew, Anna's body came flying out of the tunnel, tossed like a rag doll into the air. Her body landed a hundred yards beyond them.

Anna's funeral was pretty standard. I don't remember much of what happened at the church. Prayers were said and people spoke. The baton-twirling coach marveled how Anna never once dropped a baton. Friends spoke or shared poems. Our parents were numb.

At the graveside service the pallbearers rested the casket on two nylon straps, suspending it over the empty grave while the minister said something about Ashes to Ashes. It was a beautiful day, crisp and cold, no clouds. Cars were lined up along those little cemetery roads; the flower car was parked by the hearse.

The minister closed the graveside service with the Lord's Prayer, I remember, then took three roses from one of the many bouquets surrounding the casket. He handed one to my mother, one to my father, and one to me.

Suddenly car horns blared—not just one but every-one's—as if it were a wedding. Applause. Celebration. Car alarms went off. I looked at Dad's car, the one he and Mom and I had come in—not the family car but the vintage Thunderbird Anna loved. I stared at its front fender—at the radio antenna that stuck up there. It wasn't straight, though I was positive it had been when we reached the cemetery. Now it was twisted—that sturdy metal antenna that a circus strongman would have difficulty shaping—*it was bent into the shape of a heart.*

I thought maybe Dad had done it. But then I noticed the antennas on the hearse and the flower car—both shaped into hearts. Up and down the line of parked cars I could make out hearts on the vehicles with old whip-style antennas. Even with a heart full of pain and sadness, I couldn't help smiling. She was still at it, Anna was, my sister the spoon-bender.

# Chancey's Puppetry

Cousins Jimmy and Terry Hatch were both nine, almost ten, and were new in town. Their mothers were sisters who had bought a house together. Having lived for nine years in adjacent trailers in an Oklahoma mobile home park, they were thrilled to be living in a real New England town with wooden and brick buildings and a sense of history.

The boys came upon the shop after they stopped in at the local A&P and each bought a bag of M&Ms—peanut for Terry, plain for Jimmy. When they came out, they exited by a different door on another side of the building from where they'd entered. They were halfway through their M&Ms when they found themselves in front of a large plate glass window.

A large cardboard box decorated to make a puppet stage grabbed their attention. Two tie-dyed socks with button eyes appeared to be holding a conversation. The boys had seen puppets before and knew someone's hands, thumbs, and fingers were making the mouths move. Even so, the boys couldn't take their eyes off the puppets. They munched their M&Ms as if watching a movie.

"What are they saying?" Jimmy said.

"I don't know," Terry said. "Maybe if we listen close to the window, we can hear." They tried, but the glass was too thick.

"Why don't we go inside?" Jimmy said, straining to see around the stage. "Look at all the puppets and clowns in there."

The sign overhead read *Chancey's Puppetry*. The smaller print said: *Puppets, Clown Costumes, Party Goods, Magic.*

Inside they found organized chaos. Puppets everywhere. Marionettes, a Howdy Doody puppet, Paul Winchell's Jerry Mahoney dummy who sat on the ventriloquist's lap, Punch and Judy puppets, Kukla and Ollie without Fran, hand puppets, sock puppets, string puppets, paper finger puppets, Jim Henson Muppets. Dolls, dummies, mannequins. Clown and jester hats, wigs, rubber noses, makeup, seltzer bottles, and costumes. Puppet history and puppet instruction books, books on ventriloquism, clowning, magic, puppet ministry for churches. You could hardly see the walls. And music—calliope music like in a circus parade, not like the A&P's piped-in elevator music.

They walked to the front window to see who had been manipulating the sock puppets. No one was there. The sock puppets lay idle on the stage. In fact, no one seemed to be anywhere in the shop—no one behind the counter, no one dusting the shelves, no one arranging merchandise or straightening up.

"Check this out," Terry said, wiggling his hand into a Flying Squirrel puppet. "Hokey smokes, Bullwinkle," he said to a moose puppet on the shelf, "Whatcha doing?"

"Not much, Rock," the Bullwinkle Moose puppet answered. "What's up with you?"

"Did you see that?" Terry said, his mouth and eyes wide. "The moose moved its mouth. And it talked."

It was impossible. Terry only had his hand inside the squirrel. But the voice had been unmis-

takably Bullwinkle's, and they'd both seen its mouth move—with no hand inside.

"It must be voice activated," Jimmy said. "Try it again."

"Hokey smokes, Bullwinkle!" Terry repeated in his best Rocky imitation, moving the squirrel's mouth as he spoke. "Whatcha doing?"

Bullwinkle's mouth said, "Same as before, Rock. Not much."

The boys jumped back. They had asked the moose the same exact question—but it didn't deliver a canned response. How could that be? And how could its mouth move?

"If it's voice activated," Jimmy said, "How come it's not moving right now, when we're talking about it?"

"I don't know. Maybe it only responds to the name *Bullwinkle*," Terry, pronouncing the name *Bullwinkle* in his best Rocky voice. But the puppet didn't answer.

"Boys, may I help you?"

The boys flinched. An old man had appeared behind the counter. He looked like Geppetto, Pinocchio's creator/father.

"We're just looking," Jimmy said.

"Take your time. There's plenty to see." When the man smiled, his lips seemed very red, and one of his eyelids appeared to stick a bit too long when he winked at them.

"Can you tell us how Bullwinkle talked, how his lips moved?" Jimmy said.

"These are puppets. Some of them have minds of their own," the man said.

"Ventriloquism," Terry said. "Throwing your voice, right? You're a ventriloquist, aren't you?"

"That would seem logical," the man said. "But everything in this world doesn't always work according to logic, does it? They call me Chancey. This is my shop."

"We just moved from Oklahoma," Jimmy said. "We stopped at the A&P."

"M&M's," Chancey said, looking at the candy bags in the boys' hands. "My favorite." He smacked his lips awkwardly.

The cousins looked down at their bags. Both were suddenly empty. They hadn't been in the moment before.

Chancey stuck out his tongue. A dozen colored M&M's sat on it, some plain, some peanut. "They say M&M's melt in your mouth, but they don't in mine," Chancey said. "Not in my hand, either." He opened his hand to reveal a palm full of plain and peanut M&Ms. Then his hand closed and his mouth clapped shut.

The boys looked back down at their candy bags. Now they were a quarter full, as they'd been a moment earlier.

"You're a magician," Terry said.

"A jack of all trades, a master of none," Chancey said, giving them another wink, the lazy eyelid again hanging a bit too long.

"Well, it's a great shop," Terry said.

"Take your time," Chancey said. "There's plenty to see." It was exactly the same statement he'd made earlier. "Everything for entertaining. Clown costumes, puppets, dummies for ventriloquists, a touch of magic."

A faded publicity photo hung in a frame beside the cash register. In it sat a man with a child-size dummy on his lap.

"That's Charlie McCarthy," Chancey said.

"And who's that on his lap?" Jimmy said.

"*Who's that on his lap?*" Chancey barked. "McCarthy isn't the guy in the chair. That's Edgar Bergen behind Charlie. Bergen is there to carry Charlie and to sign the autographs. Charlie McCarthy is the star. On Bergen's lap."

"Wow," Terry said, suddenly noticing a Charlie McCarthy dummy on the shelf beside the photo. "Is this real?"

"Sure, he's real," Chancey said. "But he's not

the *original*, if that's what you're asking. There are many replicas, that fellow being one of them. They're all slightly smaller than the Real McCoy. Don't sell as many as I used to. Bergen's dead, you know. His actress daughter is Candace Bergen, who played Murphy Brown on TV. You may have seen the show."

The boys shook their heads.

"Before your time, I suppose. Anyhow, I think McCarthy's been institutionalized," Chancey said with a laugh. But when the boys shrugged, he explained, "Institutionalized. I think he lives at the Smithsonian Institute now. Institutionalized. Get it?"

The boys didn't.

"Take your time," Chancey said, and Jimmy knew what Chancey's next sentence would be before he uttered it. "There's plenty to see."

Terry, always the reader, thumbed through some of the books while Jimmy tried on a red rubber nose and a bright orange clown wig. In the mirror he looked like Larry of the Three Stooges.

"Hey, look at this," Terry whispered, pointing to a picture in a book. It was Chancey. The caption beneath it read: *The famous Chancey, created by Vaudeville puppeteer/ventriloquist Morgan Chance (born 1893, died 1956). Chancey was so lifelike and sounded so real that most people were fooled into thinking he was human.*

"Boys, may I help you?" It was Chancey behind the counter.

"I was wondering about a clown outfit," Jimmy said, still wearing the nose and wig. He motioned to the clown costumes.

"When you choose your colors, make sure they don't match," Chancey said with a hollow laugh.

"That's funny," Jimmy said, offering a weak laugh in return. "Don't want to look too GQ." Out of the corner of his eye he saw Terry sneak a peek behind the counter.

"Look," Terry gasped. "Jimmy, you've got to see this."

Chancey's head and eyes swiveled in Terry's direction and fixed on him. "What do you think you're doing?" he said. "You're not allowed back here."

By then both boys were around the counter, staring at Chancey on his stool.

"Where's the other half of him?" Jimmy said. "Where's the bottom?"

From the customer's side of the counter Chancey had seemed to be minding the shop. But now, from behind the counter, he existed only from head to waist, like a war veteran they'd seen in a parade once. Chancey, however, seemed to stop above the belt, where his navel should have been. His torso simply balanced on the stool.

"Chancey *is* real," he said. "Chancey is *real*." But when he heard himself say it, a funny look crossed his face, as if he were confused. "I *am* real," he corrected. "*We* are real," he added. His head cocked to one side then, the way a mime moves. Then he cocked it to the other side, and back, and back again, as if something inside him had malfunctioned, gotten stuck.

"If you're real," Terry said, running an arm above Chancey's head to see if someone might be manipulating him from the ceiling, "Where's your lower body?"

"I don't know," Chancey said. His head tilted forward and he looked down, like a toddler surprised to find his diaper has slipped around his ankles. "I've become separated, like Abbot and Costello going opposite directions in that horse costume." His voice didn't sound panicky; it was more melancholy, as if he realized something big had happened, but until now no one had confronted him with the reality of it.

"Who are you?" Terry asked.

"My name? My name? My name?" Chancey said, his voice slowing, slowing. "My name? My name?" It was like the battery for his voice track was running down.

Terry lifted up Chancey's shirt. There was no belt, no tee shirt, no guts—no anything. The hips were formed of a wire cage. There was no more to Chancey than a dressmaker's mannequin.

"Hey," Chancey barked. "Close the door. There's a breeze."

Terry let go the shirt flap.

Chancey giggled, then began to laugh—actually laugh—just his mouth at first, then his head, then his entire trembling torso. His eyelids opened and closed, sometimes separately, sometimes in unison.

"Morgan Chance is dead," Jimmy said. "He died in 1956, forty-five years ago."

Chancey stopped laughing, like a drunk suddenly sober.

"I just realized that," he said, his voice slow. "When you lifted my shirt. I'm not sure how I survived so long without him. Maybe it was his passion, or mine, or our love of it all—clowns, puppets, dummies, make-believe."

Chancey's head lolled onto his shoulder then and before either boy could grab him, he toppled from the stool onto the floor. He lay there behind the counter, flat as a sock puppet with no hand to give it life.

Every puppet then—every doll and dummy—began to wail. Some squeaked, some howled, others beat their chests like drums. Those with feet stomped them on shelves and floor.

The boys clapped their hands over their ears and ran for the door. They took a last look behind them, trying to make sense of it, but when wet tears streamed down Charlie McCarthy's cheeks and Howdy Doody's body started to wrack and shake, Jimmy flung open the door and he and Terry fled Chancey's Puppetry as fast as their legs would carry them.

# Beneath the Streets

On my way out of the house I stuffed my Wham-O slingshot into my back pocket. All of us had them in those days—nice solid wood, Y-shaped slingshots with thick elastic bands that had a little leather patch where you'd place your rock or heavy duty BB or whatever you were firing. Some of the kids who couldn't afford the Wham-O's made their own out of wood and others simply used heavy rubber bands stretched across forked tree branches. But Wham-O or homemade, in the late 1950s we all had slingshots.

As I had done countless Saturdays before, I headed for the two o'clock matinee at the Greenport Theater. These were the Baby Boom years and the place was swarming with kids. When the movie was over, some of the kids crossed the street to Rouse's Sweet Shoppe for ice cream sundaes, others walked down Front Street to Paradise Sweets or the Coronet for hamburgers, fries, and milk shakes. But not all of us had the money to go out after the movies, nor did we have the inclination. There was adventure to be found outside.

My friends Spider, Chuck, Ramon and I left the movies by the back exit that put us out in the alley closest to the Shelter Island Ferry terminal. My grandfather, Capt. George Broere, a locally famous sea captain, often filled in as a relief skipper there in his retirement. If my grandfather had been on, it would have meant a free ride over and back for us. But he wasn't on that day, so we turned our attention to the small sand-and-gravel beach next to the ferry slip. We tossed a few beer cans and soda bottles into the water and sank them with beach rocks loaded into our slingshots. When we tired of that, we turned our attention to our other favorite after-movies pastime: lounging in the Tunnel.

The Tunnel was a huge cement pipe accessible from the beach. We called the entire system of cement drain pipes "The Sewers," but it really didn't carry sewage. The maze was actually the underground storm drainage system for the business district. It's where the water went when it flowed down the street grates during rains and snow melts. Most of the time the maze beneath the streets lay dry and dark.

The Tunnel was about five feet in diameter, which made it impossible for us to stand up straight. The four of us had never ventured very far into it—a hundred yards from the beach opening to where it met Third Street, then a block-long run to the corner of Third and Front. Many times we had talked of mounting an expedition beyond that.

The four of us clambered into the Tunnel, which was dry, and were sitting with our backs against the walls, talking about nothing in particular when a voice called to us from the entrance.

"You looking for Tom Thumb?"

It was one of a group we called the Scary Kids. This guy had dropped out of school in eighth grade and worked at a local junk yard. He must have been 16, 17, 18 years old.

When we didn't answer, he repeated, "You looking for Tom Thumb?"

Tom Thumb was a midget, about four feet tall, maybe in his thirties or forties, who'd be described today as a street person. Nobody knew where he lived.

He had a tight little face with beady eyes. No matter if it was winter or summer, he wore a navy blue watch cap, so we never knew if he was bald or had hair under it. He had a heavy scraggly beard and a plump body. He looked like a fat-cheeked rodent: a prairie dog, a woodchuck, a weasel. Our parents had cautioned us to steer clear of Tom Thumb.

One time Chuck and I had gotten near him at Al Martocchia's Sportsman Cigar Store. He reeked of body odor. As we finished paying for our Topps baseball cards (the ones with the square of bubble gum inside) Tom Thumb hoarsely whispered, "A penny apiece for any frogs or salamanders you git me." We averted our eyes, not answering, and walked out.

"No," Ramon said to the Scary Kid. "We weren't looking for anybody. Why? Did you lose him?"

"Not hardly," the Scary Kid said. "But I been sitting over there on the dock for three hours fishing. I seen him go in there right after I set down to fish. He never come out."

"He never came out?" Ramon said. "You sure? Maybe he came out while you were reeling in a fish or baiting your hook?"

"Don't think so," the Scary Kid said. "I still got the same piece of bacon on my hook I started with three hours ago. Wasn't nothing biting, so I just been keeping my eye on this hole. I'm telling you, he ain't come out. He went in, but he ain't come out."

"You going in after him?" Spider said.

"I ain't going in there," the Scary Kid said. "Heard too many things about it. Besides, I ain't got no flashlight."

"I got one," Ramon said, pulling a penlight out of his pocket.

"I got one, too," Chuck said, and pulled one out on a key ring.

"Well then, you guys go looking, if you like," the Scary Kid said. "I wouldn't go in there if you paid me." He turned and walked away.

"All right," Chuck said. "What do we do now?"

"*What do we do now?*" I said. "It's quarter to five. I've got to be home by six-thirty for supper. Besides, I'm not worried about finding Tom Thumb. Mom and Dad said to stay clear of him."

"But what if he's in trouble?" Spider said. "What if he broke a leg and needs our help?"

"If he broke a leg, he could yell up through one of those grates to somebody on the street," I said.

"Maybe he's out cold," Chuck said. "Hit his head and can't yell. Unconscious."

"Yeah," Ramon said. "Whoever found him and saved his life would be heroes, get their pictures in the newspaper."

I could see the tide turning against me. "Maybe we should do it tomorrow," I said. "When we're not so rushed."

"But what if he really is hurt?" Spider said. "That'd be a whole day's delay getting him to a hospital."

"What if he's not hurt at all?" I said. "Maybe, maybe he lives in here, in a little apartment."

They stared at me.

"I think we better get in fast," Ramon said, getting to his feet. "A half hour in, a half hour out, and we still have fifteen minutes to get home. Deal?"

"Deal," Chuck and Spider said.

They waited for me.

"Deal," I said reluctantly.

It took only a minute to get to the first right turn up Third Street. We really didn't need the flashlights, because enough light shone through the street grates. Along the way we found twigs, branches, straw, dead grass, bottles, cans, paper, wads of newspaper, cupcake wrappers, a plastic doll's head, and plenty of loose stones and sand deposited by the runoff waters. We reached Front, the village's primary east/west thoroughfare, and followed it downtown until we reached First Street, one of two primary north/south streets.

"Time to head back," I said. "Our half hour's up."

"Yeah," Spider said. "Nobody down here but us."

I wanted to add, "Thank God," but didn't.

The words had just left Spider's mouth when we heard a high-pitched squeaking—not a screeching, but a squeaking—coming from the First Street tunnel we hadn't yet explored. Nobody moved.

"Too big for a mouse," Chuck said.

"Way too big," Ramon said. "Unless it's got a megaphone."

We laughed softly, nervously.

"Well, it doesn't make any difference," I said. "It's time to head back."

Still no one moved.

"Come on, you guys," I said. "We agreed. Half hour in, half hour out, fifteen minutes to get home."

After a moment Chuck shifted to my side. "Steve's right," he said. "We did say that."

"But—" Ramon started to object, but we heard the deep squeak again, and several softer, quieter, slightly different squeaks.

"Could it be alligators?" Spider asked.

"Alligators don't squeak," Chuck said. "Porpoises maybe, or dolphins, but not alligators."

"You think it's the guy?" Ramon said. "Tom Thumb?"

"His voice isn't that high," I said. "Chuck and I heard him in Martocchia's."

"Maybe if he was hurt," Spider said.

"If he was hurt," Chuck said, "He wouldn't be squeaking. We'd be hearing words."

"Whatever it is," I said. "We've got to get out. It's—"

"Be patient, damn it!" a voice far down the tunnel said. It wasn't exactly a yell, but it was loud, not quite commanding, but forceful.

"That sounded like Tom Thumb," Chuck said.

I thought of Tom Sawyer and Huck Finn trapped in the cave with Injun Joe. Everything about this underground tunnel told me to get out.

"Hey!" a voice said in the distance. "Slow down, damn it!"

I began backing away, but Ramon started toward the voice, Spider and Chuck right with him, drawn, I suppose, by the mystery. I went with them.

Almost immediately we hit a new junction, First and Adams. Adams Street was a short dead-end that led behind the W.T. Grant Department Store, and it seemed to be where the noise was coming from. It was darker down that corridor, so Ramon and Chuck snapped on their flashlights and inched toward the blank wall at the tunnel's end.

Ramon reached the dead-end and peeked around the corner. I heard him gasp, and we all pressed forward to see. There, in what looked like a nest—*a nest* made of straw, beach weed, leaves, and trash—lay a rat the size of a full-grown hog. It lay on its side; suckling at its huge breasts were many smaller rats. I say smaller, but each one was twice or three times the size of the largest sewer rats I'd seen. These were the size of small dogs. There were eight or ten of them.

The mother rat had huge eyes with black centers, but she didn't seem focused on us; her eyes were rolled back in her head. I had seen kittens and puppies nursing before, pushing and scrambling over each other to reach the lifeline, but it never occurred to me that sewer rats behaved the same way.

The closer I looked, the more I realized that these were not baby rats with closed eyes and untrained muscles. These were adult rats that hadn't yet attained the size of the huge one feeding them. These were capable, dangerous adult rats that could turn on us at any time.

And then we heard the voice again. "Wait your turn, damn it! Wait your turn!"

We looked and saw in the midst of the sucking rats Tom Thumb on his stomach, partially covered by the others, jockeying for position with the rest of them. The squeaking we had heard was his siblings. His was the only human voice in the lot.

I grabbed the back of Ramon's and Chuck's shirts and pulled them back.

"We've got to get out," I whispered. "Before they see us."

The others nodded vigorously.

As we turned to go, Spider said, "They're sniffing the air. Go. Go."

We reached First Street and made the turn. I made a quick check of the corridor behind us. A dark mass seemed to be clogging the bottom of the Adams Street corridor and was advancing slowly. Following the scent? They knew someone had spied on them.

"They're coming!" I whispered.

We made the hundred yards to Front Street in a flash and turned the corner onto the long straightaway that would lead us to Third Street and the homestretch.

Chuck tried pushing up on a street grate, but it wouldn't budge. "Damn. I was hoping we could climb up," he said.

"Keep moving," I croaked. "Faster."

But the cement pipe was too low for us to sprint; it was like running inside a barrel. We knew we needed to put distance between us and the army of rats pursuing us, but the best we could manage was an awkward, hunched-over, straddle run, which was exhausting. They hadn't seen us, so maybe they were advancing cautiously. But once they made the turn from First Street and saw us making the long run up Front, they'd be on us fast.

"Okay, here's the plan," I said as we ran. "The next turn's a left onto Third. Along the way we pick up rocks for the slingshots. Put some in your pockets, but not so many as to slow yourself down. If they start to close in on us, turn and fire. Maybe that'll slow them down."

We moved fast up Front Street, scooping stones as we ran. Chuck and I brought up the rear. Halfway there I heard the sound of loud hissing and squeaking. A voice yelled, "Hey, you!"

The horde had turned the corner and seen us. They looked like a blob oozing into the tunnel, except this blob was oozing faster and faster.

We passed beneath the curbside grate by the movie theater—a hundred yards to the Third Street tunnel. The rats were fifty yards behind us and gaining.

"Spider! Ramon!" I yelled. "Keep going for the Third Street turn. Chuck and I will cover your retreat. When you get there, don't make the turn. Go straight across and set yourselves up to give us cover fire. We'll leapfrog in pairs that way."

No questions asked, they took off while Chuck and I turned and waddled backwards, rapidly firing our slingshots as we went—once, twice, five, ten, twenty times each. The horde slowed its unrelenting advance only slightly.

"The turn's right behind you," I heard Spider yell.

"Get out of the way and we'll let them have it," Ramon shouted.

Chuck and I made the turn into the Third Street tunnel as Ramon and Spider began firing their mad volleys. Then, with Chuck and me barely twenty-five yards down the tunnel ahead of them, Ramon and Spider fired a final volley and followed us. All four us were out of the rats' line of sight, which was a momentary comfort, but it also meant we didn't know exactly how close they were.

"I hope you two have some ammo," Ramon yelled ahead to Chuck and me. "I'm out of everything."

"Me, too," Spider said.

"Chuck and I have BBs and ball bearings left. We'll set up at the turn to the Tunnel and hold them. You two squeeze past us there and run for the beach. Set up and grab beach stones. We'll be right behind you."

Suddenly the squeaking reached a fever pitch.

"They've made the turn!" Spider yelled. "They're in the tunnel. Closing fast on me!"

"Keep moving!" I said. My legs felt like rubber.

The next thing I knew Chuck and I had reached the final turn to The Tunnel and the beach. We set up and prepared to fire. The Third Street stretch we had just come through—with Ramon, Spider, and the rats in it—looked dark. Ramon and Spider couldn't have been more than twenty yards behind us.

"Stay in the center of the tunnel," I yelled. "Single file. We'll fire around you, off the walls!"

No sooner had I said that than Ramon came into view, then Spider.

"Let them have it!" I said, and Chuck and I began zinging ball bearings off the walls to our comrades' sides. The squealing and screeching told me we were scoring some hits. A voice—not Ramon's or Spider's—growled, "Ow! Damn it!"

Our comrades-in-arms passed us and entered the Tunnel, so Chuck and I started firing straight down the middle into the darkness now. The horde was no more than twenty feet away and closing.

"Out of ammo," Chuck said. "Time to go."

Ahead of us, Ramon yelled, "Come on! Get out! Move!"

The squeaking rose to a din. I could see it would come down to a foot race.

And then, I don't know why—he later said he had no idea why he did it either—Chuck snapped on his flashlight and shone it at the dark horde. They stopped—just for a moment, maybe blinded—and ceased their squeaking. They were still no more than huge shadows clogging the storm drain, but now I could make out eight, ten, twelve pairs of eyes, pink eyes in pairs next to each other and behind each other, all about two feet up. And there, about two feet above them—four feet tall—another set of glowing pink eyes—*Tom Thumb's*.

"Shoot for Tom Thumb," Chuck said, and I fired off the last of my ammo a little higher than we'd been shooting.

"Run!" I said, and we turned and ran.

Halfway to daylight I could make out Ramon and Spider kneeling in a skirmish line, slingshots at the ready. The beach provided an endless supply of ammo, and they were ready to hold the line until we got out.

Chuck and I stumbled out onto the beach in a scene like when the whale vomited Jonah up onto the beach. We lay there exhausted.

The horde never bothered to make the last turn that led down the Tunnel to daylight.

We told our parents right away, and the police later that night. A cop and two Road Department guys pulled up the Adams Street grate behind W.T. Grant's and dropped down into the culvert there. They found what we had described as "a huge nest," though they said it was no more than a strewn-about mess of branches, straw, grass and leaves. *Ravaged*, ravaged by the pack so they'd escape detection, I thought. No rats anywhere, and certainly none the size of a hog.

They never bothered checking out Tom Thumb. We were surprised he didn't leave town. We did our best to avoid him and only ran into him once after that, in front of Schiavoni's Bowling Alley. He was sitting on the steps when we walked past on the sidewalk.

"Hey, kids," he said, not looking up at first. "A penny apiece for frogs and salaman—" Then he looked up, stopped himself cold, and stared at us with those beady eyes. I swear, for just a second—when they caught the sunlight—his pupils glowed pink. His nose wrinkled and he sniffed the air around him.

We backed away.

"Free advice, boys," he said with a leer that exposed a picket fence of rotten teeth. "If you know what's good for you, stay above ground."

# Visitation Rights

The gorilla had been hiding in the garage all afternoon, clutching the Winters baby. The two older children called the police right after phoning their parents. Now the SWAT Team surrounding the garage had a situation.

They had no idea if the child had been harmed. They could hear only occasional crying, cooing, babbling, normal sounds for an infant. But in this case the hostage-taker couldn't be negotiated with. Sending in a portable telephone didn't make sense. This was not some thug off the streets; this was a gorilla. Funny thing was, no gorillas were missing from any of the three zoos in the state or the one across the state line, and no circuses were known to be in the area. So where had it come from?

Locating the gorilla and baby inside the garage was no problem. SWAT Team members had sneaked up to the garage's windows and shined lights in. It was sitting in a back corner between the wall and tool bench, with only part of its body exposed. The baby lay in its arms and when the baby cried, the gorilla gently rocked her. Not enough of the beast was exposed for a shot with the tranquilizer gun or a sharpshooter's rifle. Either approach was risky for the child, because a semi-tranquilized or wounded gorilla might crush the baby or tear it to pieces.

"Mrs. Winters, is there anything else you can tell us about your baby?" the Officer in Charge said asked.

"Jasmine's seven months old," she said in a strained voice. "She's been colicky since we got her. Cow's milk and even goat's milk upset her stomach, so we have to use a soy formula."

"Honey, I don't think Jasmine's diet is what the officer meant," her husband said.

"What do you mean—when you *got her*?" the Officer in Charge said. "Is the baby adopted?"

"Yes. Privately. Right after she was born. In Indiana. Our older two—our natural children—were almost through high school. After they were born, Bob and I didn't think we'd want any more, so I had my tubes tied. But last year we agreed we wanted another child, so we adopted."

"We met the mother during the interview process before the birth," Mr. Winters said. "She was a confused 17 year-old who claimed she was abducted by aliens. Really."

"Chelsea," the Officer in Charge said, turning to the daughter, "How close were you when the gorilla grabbed your little sister?"

"By the kitchen sink," the girl said. "Jasmine was in her Bouncy, her roll-around walker. She had just gone through the door from the kitchen to the living room. I didn't see the thing pick her up. I saw its back as it walked away out the sliding door to the patio. I saw its back and looked down at the Bouncy and—" Tears welled up in the girl's eyes.

"And I was playing computer games when Chelsea screamed," Steve, the older brother said. "In the den. As soon as she told me what happened, I called Mom and Dad at the Pearsons."

"Bob and I ran home and turned the house upside down first," Mrs. Winters said. "But Chelsea swore it was a gorilla. We couldn't believe it at first, so we searched everywhere."

"I prayed it had taken a doll," Chelsea said. "I wanted to believe Jasmine had climbed out of her Bouncy and was hiding in a closet."

"I know," the Officer in Charge said soothingly. "But we can see the baby in the garage. It's not a doll. And she seems okay. Nobody at fault here, Chelsea, nobody's to blame. We just have a situation to deal with. The animal control specialists from the zoo just arrived. For the moment we've got to be patient."

People gathered along the street and sidewalks. News crews were set up within fifty yards of the garage. The Officer in Charge walked over to talk with the SWAT Team Negotiator.

"The kid was adopted," he told the Negotiator. "Seven months ago. A newborn."

"Yeah?" the Negotiator said. "How's that figure in?"

"I think we ought to try to get a phone in," the Officer in Charge said. "Let you do you thing. This may not be a gorilla at all. Could be somebody in a gorilla suit."

"A snatching!" the Negotiator said, a little too much enthusiasm in his voice. "In a gorilla suit. That's a new one. Oughta make one of those video shows."

"Video shows be damned," the Officer in Charge said sharply. "I didn't say it *was*. I said *could be*. It's just a possibility. For all I know, the damned thing's a live gorilla. Neither of the kids saw its face, so they don't know if it had real eyes or those glassy costume-store ones. They saw the thing going away. To a couple of scared kids, a person in a gorilla suit walks just like a gorilla. Think about it—would an escaping gorilla look to open a door and hide inside a building? Wouldn't it look for open spaces or for a wooded area to disappear into?"

"And how did it happen upon this particular house?" the Negotiator said. "The sliding glass doors were closed but not locked. That meant this thing—or this person—would have to know the baby was inside and the parents were away. You're right. Let's get the phone in."

The Officer in Charge announced over the bullhorn that they were going to use the electric garage door opener to open the door about a foot and push a portable phone in. Then they'd close it. He invited the person in the gorilla suit to pick up the phone and begin a dialogue. Once the person in the garage raised an arm acknowledging he or she understood, the phone would come in.

A spotter radioed that he *thought* an arm had gone up, so the garage door went up a little and the phone was pushed in.

"I had a fairly open shot," one of the sharpshooters radioed. "When the door went up and the light went on, I think I had a head shot."

"Wait," the Officer in Charge said. "We don't know if it's a gorilla or a person in a gorilla suit. We give them a chance to pick up the phone and talk first."

But despite repeated bullhorn attempts to get the kidnapper to retrieve the phone, the creature remained behind the workbench with the baby. The marksmen reported that, except for rocking, there'd been no other movement.

"He may be afraid to reach for it," the Officer in Charge said. "Knows we've got our sights on him."

"Or *her*," the Negotiator said. "I'm betting it's the birth mother."

"Or *it*," said the animal handler who had been listening. "Could still be a live gorilla who doesn't understand he's supposed to pick up the phone. Maybe it only understands when you tell it to raise an arm."

The Officer in Charge said into the bullhorn, "Hello inside. Could you raise your arm for me?" He repeated each word slowly and distinctly. "Raise. Your. Arm."

No movement.

"I've got to go in," the mother said. "Let me talk to her, mother-to-mother, face-to-face. Please. Give me a chance."

The Officer in Charge and the Negotiator huddled for a minute. There were conditions. The Negotiator would accompany her, gun behind his back. So would the animal handler, tranquilizer gun behind his. And the three of them went only as far as the side door, not inside. Sharpshooters would draw the best beads they could.

Mrs. Winters explained over the bullhorn that the Negotiator was bringing her in with a bottle of the soymilk formula Jasmine needed. The Officer in Charge then asked the gorilla to raise an arm in acknowledgment.

This time, the sharpshooter radioed, he was sure an arm went up.

The three of them reached the side door and pushed it open. Before either man could stop her, Mrs. Winters reached around the door jamb and flipped on the light switch. There was a sharp *pop* and the Negotiator yanked Mrs. Winters backward, knocking the animal handler down in the same movement.

"Don't shoot!" he yelled as the three of them fell onto the grass. "Hold your fire! It's the light bulb! Just the bulb. It blew out."

"Hold your fire!" the Officer in Charge ordered.

"Let's try again," the Negotiator said, unclipping the flashlight from his belt. "This time you stay behind me, Ma'am. He turned to the animal handler. "You too."

He crept toward the open door, stepped one foot inside, and swept his flashlight beam across the garage floor. The phone lay where the SWAT Team had pushed it earlier, near a floor drain. He aimed the beam in front of the workbench, not directly on the gorilla. On the periphery of the beam he could make out the animal's hairy feet and legs.

"I hear her," Mrs. Winters whispered. "Jasmine." From the lap of the beast came a baby's cooing.

"How's the baby doing?" the Negotiator said toward the workbench, trying to sound compassionate. "Bet she's hungry."

A hissing sound, like air escaping a balloon, came from the corner then, and the Negotiator aimed his light there. Leaned up against the wall was a huge beast, the baby cradled in its arms. But before their eyes the beast began shrinking, melting away like Oz's Wicked Witch of the West.

Mrs. Winters broke free and darted forward.

"Wait!" the Negotiator cried. Too late. She was two steps ahead, and in a flash had scooped the baby into her arms. The Negotiator aimed his pistol at the gorilla, but it offered no resistance, didn't move. It simply *deflated*. There was no other way to describe it. This very real-looking gorilla was shrinking, collapsing before their eyes—not its skin, not its suit, if that's what it was, for the outside of it appeared intact—but the guts of it. The stuffing, the meat, the essence of it was melting.

Suddenly the garage door went up and the place was flooded with light and SWAT Team personnel. Two led Mrs. Winters and her baby outside to her family.

"I see the suit," the Officer in Charge said to the Negotiator. "But where's the person in it?"

"I haven't the faintest idea," the Negotiator said, shaking his head. "Not a clue."

"Hey, watch where you're stepping," the animal handler said to them, pointing at the floor. A pool of something by their feet broke apart into smaller pools and droplets, broke up and re-coagulated, then broke up again as it flowed toward the floor drain.

The Officer in Charge would later write in his report: *The substance that disappeared down the drain reminded me of the mercury I cupped in my hand when I was a kid and broke open a thermometer.*

The Negotiator would write: *The fluorescent yellow-green liquid ran down the grade from the gorilla's feet to the garage floor drain.*

Before anyone could think to swab a sample, the floor was bare, the liquid gone. A later inspection of the drain showed no trace of the substance the two officers and the animal control person described.

The gorilla suit was not a suit at all, but a real gorilla hide, like a bearskin rug. Its insides were simply unaccounted for.

The birth mother could not be located for comment.

# The Skating Party

It happened during an ice skating party at the small pond in Stirling Cemetery in Greenport. The pond had frozen over during a snap of frigid weather, which meant a bunch of us would get a bonfire going in an old car tire on the pond and set out a few kerosene lanterns around the edges for a Saturday evening skating party.

My mother drove my sister and me to the skating party. I was in eighth grade, she in seventh, so we had many friends in common. We walked through a couple of inches of crusty snow to get down to the edge of the ice. Eight or ten other kids had already arrived and more would follow.

Nothing much happened the first hour. We skated, drank hot chocolate, did some racing around. It was a dark night with a spray of stars in the sky. The moon was no more than a sliver and cast an eerie pall over the grave stones peering down over the shoulders of the pond. Since I had been at the pond for parties the two years before, any fears of attending an after-dark activity in the cemetery had pretty well disappeared. The same was true for many of my friends. However, that didn't stop us from trying to scare one another. And it didn't stop us from telling scary stories.

Larry King kicked in with a story. He was a kid who lived most of the year in Hollywood, Florida, and spent his summers in Greenport. But during this Christmas to New Year's break, he was up to visit his grandmother, so it was his first real experience with snow and ice. He wasn't much of an ice skater, but what a storyteller.

First he told the story about a greedy man whose wife had a golden arm. After she died and was buried, he dug her up and cut it off so he could hoard it. One night she came looking for it, repeatedly calling out in a scary voice that sounded like the wind, "Whooooo's gotttttt my gollllden arrrrm?" It was an old Mark Twain story we'd heard many times. But the way Larry told it there in the dark cemetery, it scared the bejesus out of us.

He also told the one about the couple in a car at Lover's Leap. At the end there's a metal hook left hanging from the driver's-side door handle, a hook like the one the escaped lunatic killer had for a hand. Again, we'd heard it before, but when Larry told it, it sure creeped us out.

Then he started with one he swore was true. The very summer before, only six months earlier, Larry had taken a shortcut through Stirling Cemetery to save time between his grandmother's house and the swimming beach at Gull Pond. It was broad daylight.

He was walking this one section we all knew at the back of the cemetery, where a little neck of land juts into the tidal mud flats like a peninsula. There are perhaps fifty or sixty graves on there. Suddenly a crow cawed above him. He looked up at it and stepped into empty air. When he came to, he found himself lying in the bottom of a fresh-dug grave. It scared him, and when he stood up, he saw all the dirt was piled on one side of the grave. He'd stumbled in from the other side. Even with the crow distracting him, he couldn't imagine how he'd missed seeing an open grave. He swore it hadn't been there in the instant before. Despite being barely five feet tall, Larry managed to climb out of the six-foot-deep grave. There was no one in it and no casket. He figured it had been prepared that morning for a late afternoon burial.

Once out of the grave, he said, he sat on the mound of dirt, surveying his situation. He was alone in a cemetery, sitting next to an empty grave, but it wasn't all that bad, because it was daylight, it was a warm summer day, and he knew he'd soon be on the beach. Nothing very scary about that, he told himself.

But then he felt a slight tremor like an earthquake. No earthquakes had ever been experienced on Long Island that he knew of. It was basically a hundred-mile-long sand bar. An earthquake didn't make sense.

"So," Larry said, "I looked down at the mound beneath me and noticed it cracking in places. It was fairly well packed, and I realized this grave hadn't just been fresh dug that day or the day before. The soil was firm; this had to be a week or two old. But little veins appeared from the tremors, like you'd see on the back of an old man's hand. I felt a trembling where my hands and rear end touched the dirt. I stood up and stepped away.

"Some small roots—they looked like roots at first—snaked out from the bottom of the pile on one end. Then some more roots, about two feet away from those others, crept out. My feet didn't want to move. I could only stare. I saw that these four or five smaller roots were connected, and it was like looking at the top of your hand without any skin on it. The roots reminded me of those hairy vines we see on the trees by the swamp, the vines we swing on. Whatever those hands were attached to—or *whoever* they were attached to—was on its stomach, like he was doing a pushup and had stretched his hands forward out of the dirt pile.

"I stepped around the open hole, putting it

between me and the dirt pile, and backed away as I tried to figure the shortest way to a road. I don't know why I didn't run right then. I was sort of hypnotized, I think, not by fear but by *curiosity*, by *awe*. Something in me just wouldn't let me leave until I saw what was there.

"The crow cawed again, which I took it as a warning. Maybe that's what it was doing when I first walked into the grave—*warning me*. It cawed again and again, so I backed up a couple more steps, putting space between me and the empty grave and the trembling dirt. Those roots started flexing the way you do when you wake up in the morning and stretch.

"As I debated which way to move, these two huge dirt-covered roots *that looked like feet*—I swear you could see the heels, or what *had been* heels at one time—pushed out the other end of the dirt pile. The distance from feet to hands must have been about ten feet, so whatever was under that dirt pile was bigger than any basketball player I ever seen, bigger than the Abominable Snowman.

"I was twenty yards away, by grave stones that said *Broere* and *Mellas* in that isolated section of the cemetery. I knew I'd have to run for either the North Road or the mud flats, but in the flats I was sure to bog down. I stood between two tombstones.

"That mound of dirt rose up like a turtle shell, like one huge dome made of baked dirt. It had to be a coating because it crumbled and dropped off as it rose up. Next thing I know there's some kind of a huge being—a yeti or whatever you call those mountain monsters, Missing Links—there on its hands and knees, shaking this huge hairy head like it was waking up from a twenty-year sleep. Judging by the length of its legs, I knew if this thing spotted me, it'd run me down in no time, so I crouched behind a tombstone with one eye on the dirt pile.

"It stood eight or nine feet tall. But it was facing the other way, away from the grave, looking down on the dirt pile I'd sat on. I shivered and prayed it wouldn't look in my direction.

"It turned, as if it sensed someone watching. I pulled my head behind the tombstone, afraid it might see me watching. I didn't move a muscle. All I could do was wait.

"But then it occurred to me—if the thing had a highly developed sense of smell, it would know I'd been nearby, on top of it and in the grave. Had it *felt* me on its back? Did I wake it up? So I hunkered down there with no way of seeing if it was coming for me, and I prayed. I prayed, hoping it wouldn't hear my lips moving."

Larry King stopped his story.

We sat waiting for a punch line like in the Golden Arm, when the narrator—after he's panned across the audience asking one final spooky time, "Whooo's gotttt my gollllden arrrrmmmm?"—snaps around and points accusingly at some listener, screaming "You got it!" so everybody jumps six feet in the air.

No punch line. Little Larry King just sat, pale as a ghost, as if he'd revisited the incident for the first time in six months, as if it wasn't a *story* but a *recollection*, as if he'd never allowed himself to hear it for fear that he might believe it.

"Yeah? And then what happened?" my sister said.

The look on Larry's face told us he'd forgotten he had an audience. It was as if he was suddenly waking up at an ice skating party in Stirling Cemetery.

"*Nothing*," he said, as if the answer surprised him too. "Nothing happened. After awhile I stood up. I didn't see anybody. I noticed there was hardly any dirt beside the open grave. I went over closer to take a look.

There were no tracks. There was nothing in the grave. It was like the thing had materialized, been created out of the dirt from the hole. Where it went from there— off to the mud flats, into town, up to the great bye-and-bye—I don't know. But I walked out of the cemetery and hitched a ride to the beach. That's all. Honest to God."

A little jeering and a few Aw-come-on remarks followed. But Larry King wouldn't recant. He stuck to his story.

"You don't have to believe it," he said. ""I'm just glad to finally have it out in the open."

While none of us believed it, a couple of the guys insisted he show us the spot. So, with Larry leading the way, we all walked to the old part of the cemetery by the mud flats.

"Will we hear a crow now?" I mocked, trying to cover my nervousness.

Larry stepped between headstones, placing his right hand on one, his left on the other. Several stones around us said *Broere* and *Mellas*.

"Right here is where I hid," he said. He extended an arm like a scarecrow. "And there is where I saw the open grave. I can't go any closer. You can go, if you like."

My sister and another girl stayed with Larry while the rest of us crunched over the dirty snow to where the empty grave would have been the summer before. We shone our flashlights on the ground.

Dead ahead we saw a tall tombstone in front of what looked like a recently filled-in grave. It had settled six inches and would need attention in the spring. The tombstone had no dates. It had only one name, *Wendigo*, beneath which the inscription read *Will rise again*. A chill ran down my spine. I remembered that *Wendigo* was an Indian name for something like a *yeti* or an Abominable Snowman, a monster that was part tree and part human. Before I could say anything, though, my ignorant friends Corey and Albert began jeering.

"Oh, yeah, right," Corey said, and Albert added, "Little Larry saw the big hairy-scary thing." And in a move that caught us all off guard, the two of them began stomping on the sunken grave.

"Take that, Wendigo!" Corey shouted.

"And that! And that! And that!" Albert taunted, jumping up and down, up and down on the grave.

"Stop it!" I shouted.

But they didn't stop, and after six or eight jumps, as their four feet landed at the same time, the grave fell in. I imagined an old, rotted casket collapsing in on its occupant. Corey and Albert suddenly found themselves up to their knees in crusty snow and frozen chunks of dirt. Their first reaction was astonishment. But then, as we stared down at them, four feet lower than the rest of us, they started to scream.

"Something's touching me!" Albert cried out.

"It's got my foot!" Corey screamed.

We all gaped open-mouthed at each other, then looked down at Corey and Albert to see if they were putting us on. Their faces told us there was nothing funny about the situation. Something was terribly wrong.

"Help!" they yelled, reaching up to us.

We grabbed on and yanked as they struggled to break free of whatever was holding them in the grave.

"Harder!" they yelled, crying now.

We pulled hard in what was a thirty-second Tug of War. A moment later they were out on firm ground. None of us waited around to talk. We lit out for the skating pond and the fire. Larry, my sister, and the other girl were way ahead of us. We caught up to them by the pond, but nobody bothered to stop for their skates or blankets. We kept going.

Once on the street we grew a little braver—a little. We stopped at the nearest house, made phone calls, and had our parents pick us up.

It was my last ice skating party in Stirling Cemetery. None of the group ever went back.

Larry King didn't visit his grandmother that summer; he stayed in Florida. Rumor had it he tried exploring the Everglades in a leaky boat and was never heard from again.

I've checked hundreds of phone books wherever I've stopped around the country, but I've never found the name Wendigo.

# Door Number Three

Harvey Hatfield noticed it when he was shaving, the wiry little hair sticking a tad too far out of his nostril. He'd never noticed it before, but today as he stood staring into the brightly lighted mirror, pulling the disposable razor across his beard hairs and rinsing off the shaving cream, he noticed it. And it bothered him. It wasn't that he was a vain man—he rated himself a seven-and-a-half on a one-to-ten scale for looks—so he wasn't unattractive. Somewhere above average, he thought. But he really didn't want to go out in public with a nose hair sticking out a quarter inch longer than it should.

He opened the medicine cabinet, pulled out a tiny pair of stork-shaped, gold-plated scissors he often used on his goatee and mustache. He got close to the mirror, lifted them to his nose and lined up on the errant nose hair. He squeezed, but heard no *snip*; the scissors wouldn't close. It was as if they were trying to cut fence wire.

Harvey tried again. Same results.

*This is difficult*, he thought, and it occurred to him that he'd never before tried to clip his nose hairs. They'd sort of taken care of themselves, like self-sharpening electric shavers did. Nose hairs had always been a low-maintenance part of his anatomy. Until now.

Harvey tried twice more, but the small scissors had met their match. He laid them on the sink, walked to his desk in the spare bedroom, and pulled out the scissors he used for paper and cardboard. He returned to the mirror, lined the scissors up on the nose hair, and squeezed.

Same result. The nose hair was like heavy gauge wire. It was like trying to cut the rabbit-ear antenna on an old TV. It wasn't actually that thick, he could see, but it felt thick. He set the office scissors next to the mustache scissors and continued shaving, mulling the matter over. As he dried his face and neck, an alternative plan formed—*yank* the hair.

Harvey pressed close to the mirror again, tried to fit his right thumb and forefinger inside a nostril that was too small for more than one digit, and tried to grab the nose hair. It was slippery and didn't stick out far enough for a good grip. He grabbed his robe off the door, slid into his slippers, and padded down to the basement. In his toolbox he found a pair of needlenose pliers. He carried them upstairs, faced the mirror again, and prepared to do battle.

*Can't hurt any more than pulling an eyebrow hair or a chest hair.* He closed his eyes, gripped the hair with the pliers, and yanked.

There was no pain. The nose hair now protruded from his nostril about two inches. But it remained attached.

"What the hell?" he said. A surprised face stared back from the mirror.

He clamped the jaws of the pliers on the nose hair again, closer to the root. Instead of a quick yank, he tried a slow, strong pull. It lengthened, so he pulled again. It came out more, almost reaching his upper lip. He'd had an ingrown whisker once and had pulled it out of his cheek. Nearly three inches of whisker hair spooled under the skin in a womb of stinky pus. He knew it could be dangerous, so he set the pliers aside and went to phone his doctor.

The receptionist advised him to come in right away. No, he should not go to the Emergency Room at the hospital; this was why he had a family doctor.

He ate his breakfast by maneuvering his cereal spoon around the low-hanging hair. When he touched it with his tongue, he found it felt sharp, like the end of a broken coat hanger. When he drank his coffee, it dipped into the liquid whenever he tilted the mug.

He was waiting at Medical Suite #3 when it opened, the first one there. Soon two other men came in and sat down. One was a blonde whose looks seemed vaguely familiar. The other was brown-haired, and his nervous smile reminded Harvey of his own.

"Tune-up?" the brown-haired man asked, looking at Harvey.

"Sort of," Harvey said with a tight-lipped smile. "You?"

"Guy problems, I guess," he said. But he didn't look down at his lap; he rolled his eyes upward toward his forehead and tapped his head. "Doc says it's all up here."

The blonde man sat quietly, eyes averted.

"How about you?" Harvey asked.

The blonde's eyes darted nervously around the room. He couldn't focus on anything. "Eye problems," he said. "I hope to be in and out fast." He dropped his gaze to the floor again.

The receptionist sat at her desk, running her finger down a page of her appointment book. Harvey expected her to call the blonde or the brown-haired man first, but she said, "Mr. Hatfield, we'll move you right along. Let me see if the examining room is ready." She disappeared down a hallway.

Harvey had been in before for routine exams—stethoscope on the chest and back, height and weight, tongue depressor and flashlight, standard things. But he'd never been in for so much as a sore throat, a cold, the flu, not even a cut finger.

A moment later the receptionist opened the door and motioned him into the hallway, saying "Last reception room on the—"

He thought she'd said, "right," but she'd turned her head when she said it. He'd nodded, believing he knew. Besides, he was the first patient of the day, so it wasn't as if he'd walk in on somebody undressing.

He walked down the hallway past several doors until he came to the last two opposite each other. He was almost certain he'd been in the one on the left. Had she told him to go in there, his usual room? Or had she said *right*, as he'd thought?

He opened the door to the right and saw that the room was considerably larger than any room he remembered. He saw four men about his age and build, all sitting in different chairs. They sat motionless, mouths open, eyes catching glints of light. Their facial features looked oddly familiar.

The heads of the two on the right hung forward; the heads of the two on the left tilted back. They didn't look dead or pale or washed out; all four looked perfectly alive, with good skin color. They didn't appear to be asleep; they just didn't move.

"Psst!" Harvey whispered. "What are you guys doing?"

None of the four answered.

Despite his growing fright, Harvey moved closer and squinted at their faces. Each had a wiry nose hair protruding from a nostril, stopping at or below the bottom lip, an inch or two farther than his own nose hair. He touched one of the men on the shoulder. The man toppled sideways and collapsed face down in a heap on the floor. Harvey stared at the back of the man's head. The scalp had been peeled back to reveal a trap door similar to the covering over a radio's battery compartment. A mass of circuits showed beneath. The man's brain resembled the guts of a computer. He pulled back the scalps of the other three to see what made them tick, too—or not tick. Same wiring. What were they? They certainly weren't human.

Harvey delicately touched his own nose hair. His mind ran through the possibilities. Had these four accidentally deactivated themselves? Or had the doctor done it when they came in for treatment? Either way, he guessed, pulling out the indestructible nose hair had been their undoing.

He stepped back into the hallway, quietly closing the exam room door behind him. He felt human, damn it. And there was a clear survival instinct in him. But he also felt a rising tide of despair threatening to drown him. Who was he? How did he fit in? If he ran, he'd need to create his own witness protection program. If he didn't, he might as well pull the damned nose hair the rest of the way out himself. His eyes alternated between the examining room door and the back exit door. What a choice.

"Mr. Hatfield?" the receptionist's voice called down the hall. "Are you lost?"

Harvey hesitated, glancing toward the waiting area. There were more men now. The waiting room was almost full. A crazy thought—a line from an old game show he'd seen in syndication—popped into his head: *I'll take Door Number Three.*

"I just remembered," Harvey said, moving toward

the entrance. "I have another appointment. The dentist or the chiropractor, I've forgotten which. But I'm happy to make room for these other gentlemen. If I don't get back later, don't worry. I'll reschedule."

Harvey put his hand on Door Number Three and left.

# Short Straw

There was a banging on the cabin door. Andy jumped up and flung it open. He was greeted by a whoosh of snow and Reuben's body—not dead, but weak—falling across the door sill.

"Cripe! Give me a hand here, Jim!" Andy yelled to me. "Pull him in. We've got to close this door."

Snow continued to gust in on the high winds. I stood weakly, and the two of us pulled our friend Reuben in and shut the door.

"Get him near the fire," I said.

We dragged him to the cabin's inadequate source of heat. We'd been snowbound for sixteen days. We'd burned every stick of furniture and torn down everything burnable within a half mile of the cabin.

The snowmobiles had long ago been buried by the blizzard, but that didn't make much difference—they were about out of fuel anyway. We'd sure miscalculated on this trip. And now it looked like it might cost us our lives.

Ten hours earlier Reuben had drawn the short straw of the three and tried to walk out of the frozen wilderness to find us help. Whether he'd been lucky to find his way back remained to be seen. He might have been better off freezing to death quickly rather than freezing slowly—and starving—with us.

We sat him as close to the fireplace as we could

without burning him. Part of me wanted him to live, but another part of me wanted him to die so the other two of us would have something to eat. We hadn't gone so far as to discuss it, but no doubt Andy and I had both entertained the idea of cannibalism. The yearning for survival is a powerful one, especially so far from the watchful eyes of civilization.

"Reuben, Reuben, you've got to stay awake," Andy said, slapping our friend's cheeks lightly. "Come on, wake up. Tell us what happened."

Reuben came around slowly. I pulled off his heavy snowmobile gloves and helped him warm his hands by the fire.

"Jesus," he screamed. "Jesus, that hurts. My hands hurt." He drew them back from the heat.

"That's a good sign," Andy said. "There's some feeling. Now tell us. What happened out there? Why'd you come back?"

Reuben closed his eyes, struggling to remember.

"The snow was thigh-high when I left here," he said. "It wasn't blowing so hard. But with the new snow and drifts, it got chest-high. I got maybe a half mile. It was such a white-out, I lost my bearings. I didn't know which way was forward, which was backward. I knew it'd be miles and miles, and you two depending on me, but with the snow piling up, I wasn't sure I'd know the highway if I saw it. I'd pass right over it.

"At first I thought I'd burrow down and make a snow cave. You know, wait out the worst of it. Then I thought, they'll never find my body if I die here. But if I could make it back to the cabin, somebody might find our bodies and learn what happened to us. So I took my best bearing on where I thought the cabin was and tried to walk as straight as I could—back. I was exhausted before I'd gone twenty-five or thirty yards.

"But then I saw the top of a tree. I didn't remember one that tall around here. But I saw the top of this tree that looked like it had the Star of Bethlehem on it. You know, like a Christmas tree? Since I didn't remember a tree like that, I figured I was going in exactly the wrong direction. I turned to go in the opposite direction—away from it—when a voice in my head said *Wait*. It wasn't like I thought *Wait*, the voice in my head actually said *Wait*. And it occurred to me—no voice this time, it just occurred to me—that maybe I could climb the tree and see where I was, maybe see the cabin, see a little bit of smoke.

"So I worked my way to the tree, and when I finally got there, it wasn't a Christmas tree at all. It was just a tall trunk that used to be a tree, and what I had thought was a shining star was a clump of ice. That's all, a clump of ice, no vision from heaven. From a distance it caught the light and sparkled. But it led me there. It saved me.

"My first thought had been to climb it, but then a clear voice inside my head—it wasn't my voice, it was another man's—said *Come inside*. I didn't know what it meant, so I began feeling around the trunk with my hands. There was a hole in it, filled with snow; the trunk was hollow.

"I set to work scooping the snow out, and after awhile there was enough room for me to get inside. The exposed surface wasn't much bigger than my shoulders to my rear end, so I built myself a little snow chair and sat there plugging the hole with my back. My knees were against my chest, my arms across my knees. I kept thinking about that phrase *born again*, and although I didn't hear it in a religious way, it occurred to me maybe this was a second chance at life—and here I was in the womb."

Reuben looked stronger, warmed by the fire. The

color had returned to his face. We gave him a little melted snow to drink.

"What happened next?" Andy said. "How'd you know to go from there to here?"

"Well," Reuben said. "I knew it'd be getting dark fast. The choices were limited. I could wait it out and probably freeze there. I could lie down and freeze in the snow. Or I could try and find the cabin again, where I could freeze to death with friends. Then I found I had a fourth choice."

"What was that?" Andy asked.

"My legs began to cramp and I needed to create a little space for myself. So I started hollowing out a little more snow, a little more snow, and after awhile my hand struck something that wasn't snow."

"What was it?" I asked.

"A bone," Reuben said. "And then a couple more. At first I wasn't quite sure what kind of bones. But then I hit little patches of clothing and realized somebody else had been in the same spot before me—maybe the man whose voice I heard in my head. I felt my way through his clothing, hoping there might be something usable there, something that could help me keep a little bit warmer, something I could use to block the door besides my own back and shoulders, to seal the entrance. The clothing was in shreds. But then I found something."

"What?" Andy said.

"A letter—in a wallet. I used the flashlight in my parka to read it. The wallet had the usual: driver's license long ago expired, credit cards, a little cash. The letter was to his family, telling how he and his companions had been caught in a storm, how he'd found the stump and hidden inside it, how much he loved them.

"He asked God to forgive him the thoughts he and his friends had had about cannibalism, for even considering they might have to eat one another's bodies as they died off. There were four of them. He was afraid he'd be the first to die, so he thanked God for helping him find the stump to hide in."

"Is that it?" I said.

"No," Reuben said, sitting up straight now, his strength returning. "There was also this." He reached into his pocket and pulled out a small gun.

"A starter's pistol?" Andy said.

"A flare gun," I said.

"Neither," Reuben said. "It's a .22 and it was loaded. My friend in the tree trunk took it so his friends couldn't kill each other."

"But how's it going to help us?" Andy said.

"We can signal for help," I said.

"That's a possibility," Reuben said. "There are five shots left. We could use two to signal and keep three for ourselves." Reuben had a strange smile on his face.

"Or we could use all five to signal," Andy said quickly, "And use none on ourselves."

"That's true," I agreed.

"Or," Reuben said, giving us a cold look, "We could save four to signal or do whatever, and use the first one—" He let his voice trail off ominously.

Andy looked at me in horror.

"What are you saying, Reuben?" I said. "Are you saying we should—"

"You both know what I'm saying," Reuben said. "The thought's crossed all of our minds at one time or another. We're starving here. We may be able to keep warm by burning the cabin board-by-board and huddling close to the fire, but we've got to eat."

"You can't be serious," Andy said.

None of us said anything for awhile.

Then Andy said, "All right then. I guess we draw straws again, don't we?"

Reuben nodded.

"Short straw out?" Andy said.

Reuben nodded again.

Andy looked at me and said, "Get the three toothpicks we used before."

I reached for the three straws.

"Just a minute," Reuben said. "Two straws. A long and a short. I was short last time. Besides, I've already died once and been born again." He brandished the gun.

"Maybe we should wait another day or two," Andy said. "We can still fire off a few signal shots. Someone might come."

"Can't wait," Reuben said. "I'm too weak. If I fall asleep, you'll jump me."

"We wouldn't do that," Andy said. "We're your friends. You know us."

"Yeah, I know you—which is why we'll do it now. Get the straws, Jim."

Reuben's words were heavy. We three had been best friends since junior high.

"God, forgive us all," I remember saying. What came to mind then was a military funeral I'd once attended, and the eerie contemplative silence after Taps. That's how it felt in that moment before I reached around for the straws.

# CAROUSEL

Angelo Potorski aimed his video camera at the whirling carousel. There were dozens of children on it, but he aimed so those coming at him were caught in the frames. He was interested in his daughters, Maria and Katrina, who sat astride two wild-looking horses that pumped up and down, up and down, as the merry-go-round spun round, his four and five year-olds hanging on for dear life.

Beside him stood his wife, Marianna, laughing and waving at the girls. Most of the other children were laughing, at least in the beginning. The younger ones, the two and three year-olds, had their parents behind them for security, holding them on. A couple of children cried. It wasn't a high-speed merry-go-round, but it was frightening enough for very small children. Once aboard, there was no way to get off—except falling—unless the man at the controls slowed and stopped it.

But the equipment operator had learned over the years that, despite all the screaming, the children's cries would eventually turn to screams of glee. There was just enough terror on the carousel, just enough fright on this most basic of rides, to get them hooked. To see children and adults on rides at circuses, carnivals, and small-town block parties was to witness fear and joy intermixed. Somehow the opposites went together.

Angelo, too, had observed the odd phenomenon

many times. Now nearly forty, he had been to many carnivals. However, he'd given up going on the rides when he was seven. He wasn't sure what he remembered from when he was younger, but he didn't want to go through it again. He hadn't wanted the girls, Maria and Katrina, to go on any rides, either, but Marianna had insisted. They needed to be like other normal children, she said. This was part of growing up. Eventually he'd given in, and here they were, watching and filming the girls in their rite of passage on the carousel, its whooping calliope piping out the background music to screams of glee and terror.

"Look at their faces, Angelo," Marianna yelled over the calliope. "Be sure to get their faces. They're having a great time."

Angelo, eye glued to the viewfinder, kept filming. *This must be their fifteenth time around. I wonder how many they get—twenty-five, thirty?* He wasn't worried about running out of film, at least not yet. This was their first ride; there would be others to film: the Teacups, the Pedal Cars, the Ferris Wheel.

Suddenly, in the viewfinder, Angelo saw Maria, the four year-old's face change. She stopped laughing and a look of terror came over her. He wasn't sure he'd seen it at first, but when she flashed past again, he saw it even more clearly—her wide eyes, her face contorted.

*She's ready to cry*, he thought. But when she flew past again, she wasn't crying. She was screaming. Something had changed for her, and on the next pass Angelo saw Katrina's face had changed, too. For one moment, as Maria's wooden horse rose and Katrina's dropped, their mounts appeared in tandem in the viewfinder, the wild-eyed horses' sneering lips curled back to reveal gnashing teeth, their angry nostrils snorting steam. The ride seemed to speed up.

"What's wrong?" Marianna cried over the calliope.

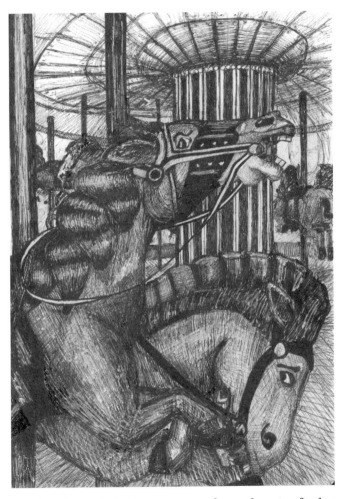

Angelo pulled his eye away from the viewfinder and watched his girls spin past, bobbing up and down as their horses circled the centerpost. He saw his screaming daughters clutching the silver support poles which skewered the horses like straight pins skewering butterflies in a collection.

"What's happening?" his wife screamed.

"I don't know," Angelo said. He put his eye back to

the viewfinder, not knowing why, and caught the girls in a frame again. This time he saw something—a flash, a split-second image—that reminded him of his childhood. He kept filming and when the girls came around again, he saw what he'd feared—two hunched things with hideous faces and wings, *gargoyles,* one riding each girl's back. He felt sick to his stomach. Bitter terror rose in his throat.

Something, some word, escaped his lips, because Marianna yanked at his arm, demanding, "What? What did you say? What did you see?"

He didn't answer. He kept his eye glued to the viewfinder. The gargoyles' faces and bodies were gray as tombstones, their wings brown as fresh-turned earth from a grave. Fangs—like those he'd seen in a vampire movie—hung down to their chins.

The other children screamed now—not with glee but in terror, none of them laughing—except those smallest of innocents with parents behind them, parents unaware what was happening around them. Surprise. Confusion. They seemed to see nothing.

Each time Maria and Katrina passed by—Marianna screaming in his ear, the carousel picking up speed—Angelo watched as the winged gargoyles on his daughters' backs tried to sink their clawed feet and wicked fangs into the girls' thick shoulder and neck cords.

*Harpies!* That was the word he'd cried out a moment earlier, the word his wife had heard him utter. Not *gargoyles. Harpies!* He'd read about them in *The Odyssey,* or was it *The Aeneid?* Didn't matter. Suddenly his daughters' pleading eyes and screaming voices brought it all back. He could feel their clawing and scratching and biting on his own shoulders and neck—not now, but then, when he was seven and riding the merry-go-round. It came back fresh, the terror he'd felt when he looked out and saw his mother and father on the sidelines, saw them every time he flew by, their faces confused, frightened for him, wondering why their boy and the other children were screaming, screaming on the careening ride.

He'd been powerless to do anything at seven except clutch the shiny metal pipe that reminded him of the pole firemen slid down in the fire station to save time. He had to hold onto that pipe for dear life or be thrown from that snorting, fire-breathing steed of Satan. And the outward motion, the centrifugal force, would thrust him into the outer darkness where—he wouldn't be able to help himself—he'd hit his head and die. His only other choice was to hang on, to hang on and ride out the harpies, outwait them, to hope and pray the man at the controls would stop the ride.

That's what his daughters were going through at four and five. They were learning about decisions, learning about fear and faith, learning to hang on. Filming, filming. Filming, filming as the ride went round and round and round and the children screamed and screamed. Finally—he didn't know how many revolutions later—the ride slowed. Angelo could hardly believe what he saw in the viewfinder. As the bobbing horses slowed to a stop, the harpies—like the grotesque winged monkeys in *The Wizard of Oz*—lifted from the backs of his daughters and the others and simply evaporated.

Parents raced from the sidelines to reclaim their children, to calm and comfort them. There were mutterings. "Going to sue these people." "Incompetence." "Drunken machinery operator." "Psychological damage." "Counseling."

Angelo slid the camera into its shoulder case and hurried with Marianna to rescue their daughters. It took awhile to calm the girls down. Angelo suggested ice cream, but no one was in the mood yet.

The girls told of something biting and scratching them, though their skin showed no marks.

"It just got going too fast," Marianna told the girls. "It scared you." Then to Angelo she said, " It felt like the ride was out of control. It scared them. Not just our girls, but the others, too."

Angelo knew it wasn't that simple, but he didn't argue. He doubted his wife would believe him if he told her about the harpies.

*Wait,* he thought. *This time I've got it on tape.* But his hope faded as quickly as the harpies had evaporated. He knew when he replayed the tape at home, it would show nothing but scared kids on a carousel. What remained to be seen wasn't the videotape, but whether his daughters would vow, as he did at seven, to never again ride the carousel.

# The Camp

A simple break-in, that's all we planned. We were looking to get some money to buy booze and cigarettes, so we figured a basic home invasion was the way to go. Well, not a real home; we'd break into a summer camp. Might be a little cash in a drawer. Nobody ever left any expensive jewelry or anything, but usually there was something we could pawn off pretty quick—stereo, microwave, TV—to make fifty or a hundred bucks. Then, of course, since we were minors, we'd need somebody else to buy the beer and cigarettes for us.

So we targeted Squanto Pond, because we knew nobody would be up there so late in the year. If anybody was around, it'd just be for ice fishing. Even so, the camps weren't much in use; the ice fishermen tended to come in by snowmobile and went out the same day.

There were about fifty camps around the pond. Some were nice, some pretty ratty, some you wouldn't put trailer trash in.

The lake was maybe a mile end to end. We parked just off the access road and hoofed it in. It didn't occur to us that if we picked up anything big, like a stereo or a microwave, we'd have to lug it all the way back out to the car. Chalk that up to our inexperience. We'd only done a few break-ins and my partners weren't known as the sharpest knives in the drawer.

Benny dropped out of high school when he was a freshman. And Gregor—whose real name was Gregory, but Gregor sounded cooler than Greg—had dropped out when he was a sophomore. I hadn't dropped out; I was just hanging around with these guys, taking another day off from the grind of tenth grade. If my parents knew I was skipping school, they'd have been mortified, and it they knew why I was skipping, yeouch.

We walked past three or four prospective targets. When we got to a red cedar building about forty feet by thirty feet, with a nice deck overlooking Squanto Pond, we knew it was the place. There was no smoke from the chimney and we didn't see any tracks going into or out of the place. The snow was hard and crunchy enough that we didn't worry too much about our own tracks. It would likely be spring before any break-in was discovered, and if it was reported at all—many of the camp-owners didn't bother, they just complained, because the follow-up from the police wasn't so good— by the time anyone investigated, the snow would be melted and any tracks gone.

Gregor used a small pry bar to pop the back door, then put his shoulder to the inside door to force it. It didn't take much. It was one of those simple locks, and when the door popped, there was hardly any damage. In fact, we were able to close it behind us, the latch barely catching.

What surprised us was that it was warm inside. The place had electric heat, and the power hadn't been turned off. We snapped on the lights. The clocks on the microwave and on the wall were both running. The place had a nice kitchen and looked like it could have been lived in year-round. The thermostat read 68 degrees.

"Crap," Benny said. "You think somebody's living here?"

We spread out, took a quick look around, didn't see anybody.

"Doesn't matter," Gregor said. "Let's take what we need and get out. And if there is somebody living here, maybe there's some cash or jewelry."

"This just doesn't feel right," I said. "It's one thing to burglarize a summer camp, but a place where somebody's living? What if they come back while we're here?"

"They won't," Gregor said. "There were no tracks in or out, no sign anybody's been here for awhile. My guess is, somebody left it after foliage season and forgot to turn off the electric and drain the pipes." He lifted a finger and pointed at the kitchen sink, which had a slight drip.

"Or maybe a renter skipped out without telling the landlord," Benny said.

We stood looking at each other for a minute. Things didn't make much sense, no matter how much Gregor and Benny tried to explain them.

"I think we ought to just get out of here," I said.

"We're already in," Benny said. "We may as well take advantage of it and then get out. Spread out."

There were four rooms and a bathroom, so it was easy to check out. Benny took the bathroom and the kitchen/dining area, Gregor took the two bedrooms, and I took what looked like the family room. Mine was the largest in the house, with a fireplace, sofa, three easy chairs, and a pool table. There were paintings of naked women on the wall. They weren't pornographic or obscene; they were nudes in the sense of the Greek or Roman paintings, although they weren't from those times. These were modern nudes—eight of them.

I made my way quickly from one painting to the next, checking behind them for a safe—as if I'd have known what to do if I found one. Unless it was unlocked,

I'd have no chance of getting into it. It didn't matter; there was nothing but wall behind the paintings. I spotted a huge television, but I knew there was no way I could lug it out; even the three of us together would find it difficult. I checked the drawers of the end table, the coffee table, and the buffet next to the fireplace.

"Find anything?" Gregor called from the bedroom doorway.

"Nothing but a well-used microwave," Benny said from the kitchen. "It's filthy."

"No jewelry in the bedroom. No cash either," Gregor said. "Anything in the big room?"

"Nothing I can find," I said, and proceeded to look for change in the couch cushions.

"Never mind that," Gregor said. "I don't mean chump change. I mean something of value."

Suddenly the paintings caught their eyes.

"Wow!" Benny said. "Look at those."

"Far out!" Gregor said. "Who do you think these broads are?"

"I don't think they're broads," I said. "I don't think they're locals at all. I think these are paintings of models who sat for famous artists."

"Oh really, Mr. Smarty Pants?" Benny said. "Looks to me like they're all painted by the same person."

I looked at the paintings again. He was right. All eight paintings had a similarity to them, something that connected them, a style, a brush stroke, the way the women were posed, a similar sense of color, something that said they were all painted by the same artist.

"They were done here," Gregor said. "In this room. Look at the backgrounds."

He was right. Each had been painted somewhere in the room, near the fireplace with a fire going.

"So now we know, whoever owns the place is a painter," Benny said.

"Maybe," Gregor said. "But I didn't see paints. No easel, no canvas. Nothing about it says a painter lives here."

"Maybe the painter shoots photographs here," I said, "and then paints from the photographs elsewhere. My Uncle Harry does it. With the sun always changing, it's hard to paint at some locations, so he shoots a picture. Or if he's traveling and sees something he wants, he takes a snapshot he can paint from later."

"Makes sense," Gregor said.

The two of them walked over to the pool table.

"Want to play?" Benny said.

"We haven't got time," I said. "We've got to get out before somebody comes back."

"Nobody's coming back," Gregor said. "Let's play. Benny, you rack. Round-robin nine-ball."

"Wait a minute," Benny said. "Look at those paintings. I heard somebody say this about the Mona Lisa, that famous painting—her eyes follow you all around the room. That's what these do. Look at them. Wherever you go, they watch."

We began moving around the room.

"Yeah," Gregor said. "Ain't that weird?"

"It's pretty neat," I said. "I don't know if it's a painter's trick or what, but it seems pretty neat."

"Yeah? Well, it creeps me out," Benny said.

"Aw, come on. Let's shoot some pool," Gregor said impatiently. "It's warm in here. Nobody's around. We can hike out later. This way the day won't be a total loss."

The three of us walked back to the pool table.

"Grab the corners on that cover," Gregor said. "Peel it back to this end and throw it in the chair."

Benny and I each grabbed a corner of the huge sheet covering the pool table and pulled it back.

"Holy crap!" Gregor said.

We stopped and caught a glimpse of the terror in Gregor's eyes as he stared at the exposed table. There lay a naked man, white as a sheet, face-up in a bath of silvery liquid. There was no green felt cover like on a normal pool table; there was nothing but the liquid with the man floating in it. The only parts of him above the surface were his toe tips, fingertips, navel, and face.

"What the hell?" Benny said.

We stood there as if our feet were glued to the carpet. I wanted to scream, but I couldn't take my eyes off the man who looked like he'd been frozen in the ice. Except this wasn't ice. It was some kind of silvery liquid. Not water. Mercury? Not exactly mercury, either, because it was clear enough that it had to be partly water.

"Who do you think he is?" Gregor said. "Is he dead?"

"I don't know," I said. "Benny?"

"I don't know," Benny said. "I can't tell. He doesn't smell."

"That's because he's underwater," Gregor said.

"What are we supposed to do?" I said. "Should we call the police?"

"No," Gregor said. "We don't want to get involved in this. If we call, they'll come out and investigate. And if we call anonymously—before our tracks melt away—they may figure out who we are and connect us with it, think we did something. It won't work. We just need to get out of here."

I couldn't take my eyes off the body in the pool table.

"He couldn't have pulled the cover over himself," Benny said. "Somebody else must be involved."

"You're right," I said. "So somebody could be coming back. Let's cover him up and get out."

Benny and I pulled the cover back over the pool table and arranged it the way we found it.

"Wait," Gregor said. "We can't leave the cover. It's got fingerprints now. We'll take it with us."

"But what about everything we touched?" Benny said.

"We haven't touched much. Remember where you went and start wiping," Gregor said. "There's a roll of paper towels there by the sink. We'll take the paper towels and pool table cover when we leave."

We spent five minutes wiping down every surface we could remember touching. After I had wiped the end tables, coffee table, and buffet, I went to the paintings and wiped the frames all the way around. Each time I moved a painting, in the back of my mind I heard a tiny eek, a little scream, no louder than a mouse. I was in a hurry and didn't have time to think about it. But each picture I went to gave that eek sound. When I finished, I stood in the center of the room, looking for any spot I might have missed. I felt the eyes of the women on me.

"You guys," I said. "Come here."

The two of them came back into the big family room.

"You done?" Gregor said. "We finished ours."

"Just stand here a second," I said. "Listen. See if you hear a noise, even a very faint noise, coming from the paintings."

The three of us stood there a full thirty seconds but heard nothing.

"Okay," I said. "Now go up to one of those paintings—use your sleeve so you don't leave a fingerprint—and try moving the frame. Move it a little and see if you hear anything."

Gregor walked to a painting and moved it. "I see what you mean," he said. "It's like a squeak. The painting's not on a hinge, so it's not that kind of a squeak. It's almost like a—"

"A voice," Benny said as he moved a frame. "It sounds like a voice."

He and Gregor touched another painting.

"I don't know what it is," I said. "But it's pretty creepy. It's time to hit the road."

Gregor and Benny headed for the door.

"Wait a minute," I said. "The paper towels. Put them in a bag so we can take them with us. And what about the pool table cover?"

"Maybe we could just wipe it," Benny said as he threw the paper towels in a paper bag.

"No," Gregor said. "Take the cover. We'll burn it later."

"But if we take it," I said, "We've got to—you know—look at *him* again."

"We'll make it fast," Gregor said. "Rip it back, fold it up, and get the heck out. Ready? Go!"

Benny and I grabbed the cover, peeled it back quickly, folded it once, then again and again, trying not to look at whoever or whatever was under it. We never folded a sheet or a blanket as fast in our lives. I stood there with it under my arm.

"Jesus," Gregor said. "Did you feel that? The temperature must have dropped ten degrees just now."

He was right. And it hadn't dropped slowly, as if we'd changed the thermostat; it dropped while we were folding the cover.

We stared down at the man in the silver pool whose surface rippled now. His eyelids snapped open, the centers of his eyes looking like my grandmother's cataracts, huge and cloudy. He didn't blink.

We all tried to yell out, but before we could, all hell broke loose as women began screaming around us, wailing and crying "Oh no!" and "Help!" and "Save me!" from the paintings which trembled and shook, tilting this way and that, wooden frames clattering as they threatened to loose themselves from the hooks they hung from. The silvery liquid rippled wildly, as if an earthquake was gaining strength somewhere deep below.

I looked at Gregor and Benny, who had clapped their hands over their ears.

"Get out now!" I shouted, and we were out the door in a second, sprinting across the snow in our heavy boots.

When we got to the car, Benny had the bag of paper towels, but I didn't have the pool table cover. I don't know if I carried it some or all of the distance or if I dropped it on the floor in the big room. I have no memory of it.

We drove as fast as we could for twenty minutes, then stopped at a diner to warm up with coffee, get rid of the jitters, and talk about what we'd do. After an hour we decided to call the police. They sent an officer to talk to us at the diner. He called for a second person to go to the camp with him. We wouldn't go, but gave the cop our names and addresses.

They found the paintings on the floor where they had fallen and they found the pool table with its holding tank—the cover over it—but there was no body in the liquid. Wet footprints led out of the room to the porch. But that was as far as the footprints went. The person had vanished into thin air.

There were no bodies, no blood, no crime scene except for our breaking and entering, which was by our own admission. If the man's fingerprints had been on the paintings, I had wiped them off. We later get off with a misdemeanor.

The paintings matched the photographs of eight women reported missing over a four-year period. A recording on the message machine at the camp asked respondents for the Models-Wanted-to-Pose-for-Artist ad to leave their names and phone numbers, and the artist would get back to them. Two women had left their information. When the cops checked on them, they were safe. So maybe we saved a couple of them. No bodies were ever found, either the eight women's or the man's.

Gregor and Benny started a trash hauling business.

I returned to high school and finished. Then, surprisingly, I went on to become a minister. I figured if there really was a cosmic battle of Good and Evil going on, I wanted to be closer to the one side than the other.

# Neighborhood Watch

Angus McPherson was the first to notice the broken window in the factory building. He was on Neighborhood Watch that night with Tommy Trotter, who most people called Pony because of his last name.

"Hey, look at this," Angus said, calling Pony over to the window.

They very seldom had any action during the Neighborhood Watch, which they and their neighbors had formed ten years earlier to keep the area safe. But occasionally something would turn up. Usually it wasn't burglars they called in about, it was suspicious people, like a car prowling the neighborhood at night. Most often it turned out the "perp" was simply someone looking for a house number in the dark.

In the ten years Angus and Pony had been walking their beat, occasionally with other partners but most often together, they'd developed a close friendship. They never accosted any criminals, and the closest they came was chasing some kids off the church steps when they loitered too long.

"Looks like it's been broken from the outside," Pony said. "No glass out here. All the glass goes in."

They used their flashlights to check the sill lock on the window. It was still locked.

"Maybe it's just a broken window, as simple as that," Angus said. "A baseball or a rock would do that."

"Or," Pony said, "Maybe somebody broke it, reached in and opened it, climbed in, and locked the window behind so it'd look like nobody broke in, so we'd walk on by and not report it."

"You got a point there," Angus said. "I'll call it in." He pulled out his cell phone and dialed the police. Nancy Diller was on dispatch and took his call.

"I've got an officer at a traffic stop nearby," she said. "I'll have him there in five minutes. Don't go in. Just stay near."

Angus and Pony checked out the building a little more closely while they waited for the cop. No sign of entry or exit in any other parts of the building. They shone their flashlights through the broken window again, scouring the area inside to see if anything was out of the ordinary.

"Everything looks okay," Pony said, "Unless some-body's gone inside to one of the offices or something."

The two men stepped back, crossed the street and took the long view.

"Any lights on?" Angus asked. "Maybe a wiggling flashlight?"

Neither of them saw anything. They looked up and down the street, hoping for the cop's headlights. By now the dispatcher would have also notified the building's owner, who would probably come down, too. The two men, both in their early seventies, were in fair physical shape and expected to take part in any search of the premises. Even though they weren't armed, they could offer some sort of backup.

"Hey, is that smoke up there?" Pony said, shining his light toward the top of the building.

"Where?" Angus said. "I don't see anything."

"Right there," Pony said, pointing a finger at some-thing that looked like thick steam or factory exhaust. It showed pure white over the flat roof. If not for the moonlight, the two men wouldn't have seen it.

"I see it now," Angus said. He stared at it a moment, then scanned the street again for headlights. Still none.

"Should we call in a fire alarm?" Pony asked. "I mean, what if there's a fire while we're waiting for the cop? Even if it's a false alarm, at least we'll have it checked out."

"I guess we'd better," Angus said. He pulled out his cell phone, dialed Nancy in dispatch and told her what they'd seen. She promised them a couple of fire trucks in no time.

"Looks like we're getting some action tonight," Pony said, gripping the nightstick he'd bought at the Army-Navy Store. He'd been carrying it the ten years they'd been on Neighborhood Watch, but he'd never used it except to rattle it across the picket fences—bappa bappa bappa—the way he had when he was a kid. The banging had taken the finish off the stick and left many nicks. The other time he'd taken it out was when they rousted the kids from the church steps.

"Each mark," he'd said to the kids with mock seriousness, "came from a smack on somebody's head."

The kids laughed nervously, thanking them for keeping the neighborhood safe. Angus heard them talking under their breath as they dispersed—saying what old fools these two decrepit men were. But that was all right. These were just school kids who'd grown tired of being told by adults to move along.

"That's flames," Pony said, pointing his flashlight at an upstairs window.

"It's a reflection on the window glass," Angus said, squinting. "Right below where the smoke's showing. Must be a fire in the upstairs room."

"What'll we do?" Pony said. "What if there's someone in there?"

"There shouldn't be anybody there now," Angus

said. "Everyone's gone home. No cars around. The place should be empty."

"Unless there's a burglar," Pony said. "What if somebody did go in that window and they're upstairs caught in the fire?"

"And what if the person who broke in set the fire?" Angus countered.

"Okay," Pony said. "So you think the burglar will run out soon? Maybe out that door by the broken window?"

"Or the door on the other side. There's only two obvious exits," Angus said.

The two men stood rooted by their indecision.

"Maybe it's not a burglar," Pony said. "Maybe it's a homeless person—or two or three or five. Maybe it's a bunch of kids having a party. They could be in trouble."

"There's no screams. They'd scream if they were in trouble," Angus said. "I think we should wait. The Fire Department will be here any minute."

"You know as well as I do," Pony said, "A minute could make the difference."

Angus looked at his friend, blinked, and said, "You're right. Let's go."

When they reached the broken window, Pony unlatched and opened it. Angus got down and made himself into a bench so Pony could climb inside. Once in, he opened the door for Angus. They flashed their lights until they found a light switch that lit a staircase. They began the long climb, yelling as they went, "Fire! Fire! You've got to get out."

At the top of the stairs they found a long hallway. They raced toward the room where they'd seen the fire. Suddenly the overhead sprinkler system kicked in, showering them with a blanket of water.

"Took its own sweet time coming on," Angus yelled, and the two of them pulled their jackets over their heads and felt their way along the wall until they bumped into a door.

"It's locked," Pony said. He knocked hard. No one answered.

"What now?" Angus said.

Pony felt the door. "It's not hot," he said. "It sounds hollow. Let's pop it fast, get in and get out." They heard a siren in the distance, but didn't know if it was police or fire.

"We both put our shoulders into it at the same time," Pony said. "A quick look then out. As soon as it opens, keep behind me and stay low. If there's black smoke up high, it'll choke us."

Their shoulders hit the door and it popped open, their momentum carrying them into a room the size of a small gymnasium. Through the sprinkler water Angus and Pony saw a huge bonfire in the center of the room, not on a hearth but on the bare wood floor. Its flames licked upward.

In a circle around it sat seven children—or were they midgets?—legs crossed Indian style, their black hoods making them look like tiny priests. They held their hands in front of them as if praying, oblivious to the drenching water. As fast it quenched the flames of the bonfire—a bonfire which had no fuel, no wood, no rags, no combustibles, a fire *ex nihilo*—just as quickly the flames sprang back, challenging the water and converting it to steam.

"Hey, kids! You've got to get out!" Angus yelled. "The place is burning down around you."

But it wasn't burning down around them. It was burning within their circle.

None of the seven answered.

The fire burned orange and white, with no black smoke, not even gray. Only pure white—was it steam?—exited the three-foot hole in the roof. Angus would later report: *No black smoke, only intense fire and heat. Pure white smoke, maybe steam, went up the chimney.*

"Is that chanting?" Pony said.

Through the crackling of the fire Angus heard a steady hum, a single note. Each voice was different, but the chorus pitched the one deep note.

"They're hypnotized," Pony said. "In a trance."

All at once, in perfect unison, the seven shifted to a higher note. The flames danced higher, licking the roof rafters.

Pony advanced on the closest figure and reached a hand to his shoulder to shake him. A spark jumped from the shoulder to Pony's fingertip. He drew back.

"He shocked me!" Pony said. "Like an electric fence."

"Hey!" Angus screamed into the circle. "Hey! Get out! It's not safe!"

The voices rose another note.

Angus grabbed Pony's nightstick and touched a hooded figure on the shoulder. It ignored him and the seven kept focused on their note and the fire.

Pony picked up a chair and tossed it into the circle. It snapped and disappeared like a mosquito in a bug zapper.

For a split second one figure turned in their direction. Sparks shot from its eyes. Then its focus was back in the circle.

"Holy Mary, Mother of God," Pony said.

No sooner had he uttered the words than all seven turned and glared at the old men.

"Heaven help us," Pony cried out. "Can you feel that, Angus?"

"It feels disgusting," Angus answered. "The air's thick with something vile. I believe, my friend, we've come face-to-face with Evil."

They could see that the seven children staring at them were not children at all. The faces were melting in the heat, oozing, dripping like wax onto their laps to reveal huge black eyes and jaws that protruded like insects' mandibles.

"Sweet Jesus, will you look at that?" Pony said.

The fire flared and a blast of heat knocked Angus and Pony backwards toward the hall door. The seven turned their attention back to the fire and a new note, moving up through a series of four more notes in rapid succession. The flames licked higher, and more white smoke billowed out the roof hole. But the hole couldn't handle it now—as if a chimney damper had suddenly closed—and the white cloud widened to fill the upper part of the room with smoke. Sparks shot from the cloud's underbelly.

"We've got to get ourselves out," Angus said, and he grabbed Pony by the arm and yanked him into the hallway. The door slammed shut behind them with such force that it cracked. Angus and Pony got to their feet and staggered toward the stairs.

Whoosh! The sound came from inside the room, as if the air had suddenly, violently, been sucked out of it. After the whoosh came a Wham! Both men would later describe the second sound as a sonic boom, the thunderclap a jet makes as it breaks the sound barrier. Then everything was still.

Two firefighters shouldered the door open not a minute after the whoosh and wham. They found no one. And no fire. No smoke. Nothing charred. However, everything in the room—chairs, tables, tool chests, a seven hundred pound workbench with iron vise—lay overturned. The room looked as if a tornado had struck. The three-foot hole in the ceiling no longer existed. Now almost the whole roof was torn away. No children—and no bodies—were found anywhere.

It was six months before Angus and Pony returned to the Neighborhood Watch. Pony, convinced that his religious words had saved them by rushing the chant, turned to wearing a crucifix. Angus strapped on a nightstick like Pony's. They talked about the night over and over. But before long they were dragging their nightsticks along the fences—bappa bappa bappa— praying for another night that would quicken their hearts.

# O R D E R   F O R M

**Burt Creations**

PLEASE SEND ME THE FOLLOWING:

| QUAN. | ITEM | PRICE |
|---|---|---|
| _____ | **A Christmas Dozen** Hard Cover Book ($17.95) | _____ |
| _____ | **A Christmas Dozen** Paperback Book ($14.95) | _____ |
| _____ | **A Christmas Dozen** Double cassette ($15.95) | _____ |
| _____ | **A Christmas Dozen** Double CD ($16.95) | _____ |
| _____ | **Unk's Fiddle** Paperback ($13.95) | _____ |
| _____ | **Odd Lot** Paperback Book ($14.95) | _____ |
| _____ | **Even Odder** Paperback Book ($14.95) | _____ |
| _____ | **Oddest Yet** Paperback Book ($14.95) | _____ |
| _____ | **Wicked Odd** Paperback Book ($14.95) | _____ |
| _____ | **Odd/Even/Oddest/Wicked** Four Pack ($54.80) | _____ |

*Shipping & handling is $4.50 first item, $2.50 per additional item. Connecticut residents add 6% sales tax.*

SALES TAX _____

SHIPPING _____

TOTAL _____

**FREE SHIPPING** ON ORDERS OF MORE THAN 10 UNITS

NAME

ADDRESS

CITY                    STATE                    ZIP

TELEPHONE          FAX          EMAIL

**PAYMENT:**

❑ Checks payable to: **Burt Creations**
   Mail to: 29 Arnold Place, Norwich, CT 06360

❑ VISA ❑ MasterCard

Cardnumber:_____

Name on card:_____

Exp. Date: _____(mo) _____(year)

◼ **Toll free order phone** 1-866-MyDozen (866-693-6936 / Secure message machine) Give mailing/shipping address, telephone number, MC/Visa name & card number plus expiration date.
◼ **Secure Fax orders:** 860-889-4068. Fill out this form & fax.
◼ **On-line orders:** www.burtcreations.com
                     order@burtcreations.com

www.burtcreations.com